The Fifteen Streets

Rob Bettinson

A SAMUEL FRENCH ACTING EDITION

SAMUEL FRENCH
FOUNDED 1830

SAMUELFRENCH-LONDON.CO.UK
SAMUELFRENCH.COM

ISBN 978-0-573-01688-2

www.samuelfrench-london.co.uk

www.samuelfrench.com

FOR AMATEUR PRODUCTION ENQUIRIES

UNITED KINGDOM AND WORLD
EXCLUDING NORTH AMERICA
plays@SamuelFrench-London.co.uk
020 7255 4302/01

Each title is subject to availability from Samuel French,

depending upon country of performance.

THE FIFTEEN STREETS

First presented at the Belgrade Theatre, Coventry in February, 1987. It was subsequently produced at the Playhouse Theatre, London, on 20th May, 1988, by Philip Talbot and Pamela Hay for Talbot Hay Productions Ltd and The Fifteen Streets Ltd, with the following cast:

John O'Brien	Owen Teale
Dominic O'Brien	Nigel Miles-Thomas
Mary Ellen O'Brien	Margo Stanley
Shane O'Brien	Paul Haley
Katie O'Brien	Faye Dannell/Kim Dormand/
	Helen Morland/Karen Wiseman
Molly O'Brien	Tara Moran
Mick O'Brien	Ian Tucker
Peter Bracken	Patrick Holt
Christine Bracken	Allison Dean
Hannah Kelly	Sheila Tait
Nancy Kelly	Lorraine Murrin
Joe Kelly/Father O'Malley	Neil Phillips
Mary Llewellyn	Christine Nagy
James Llewellyn/Father Bailey	Frank Harling
Beatrice Llewellyn/Bella Bradley	Pamela Buchner
Peggy Flaherty	Lyn Douglas
The Music Man	Peter Yates
Doctor	Alan Collins
Market Drunk/Man with cart	Geoff Lawson
Maid/Neighbour	Deborah Padfield
Neighbour	Jill O'Hare
Neighbour	Jan Younger

Directed by Rob Bettinson
Designed by Adrian Rees

The action of the play takes place in an area called The Fifteen Streets

Time—1910

CHARACTERS

John O'Brien
Dominic O'Brien
Katie O'Brien
Molly O'Brien
Mick O'Brien
Shane O'Brien
Mary Ellen O'Brien
Hannah Kelly
Joe Kelly
Nancy Kelly
Peggy Flaherty
Bella Bradley
James Llewellyn
Beatrice Llewellyn
Mary Llewellyn
Father O'Malley
Father Bailey
Peter Bracken
Christine Bracken
David Bracken
The Group of Kids
Doctor
Maid
Drunk in market
Woman in market
Removal Man
Musician (optional)
Neighbours, crowd, servants, stretcher-bearers, etc.

PRODUCTION NOTES

Period

The story takes place in 1910, in an area called The Fifteen Streets which was in the location of Tyne Dock, between South Shields and Jarrow on the south bank of the Tyne.

Set

The set for the play should be a conglomerate consisting of composite images which combine as one to convey the period atmosphere and environment. The story unfolds in the audience's imagination sparked by the images they see on stage. If the set does not have the versatility to utilize this with speed and style and gets bogged down in heavily detailed realism then the massive theatrical moments like the drowning of Katie in Act II will not work.

In the original production there was a small forestage area which extended into the auditorium, rather like an apron. This was logged and structured to represent a dock-cum-wharf, and extended the full width of the forestage left and right to form pier ends. The style of the rest of the basic set echoed this dock feel. There were two raised areas downstage right and downstage left. These were as close to the iron as possible. These downstage levels were joined by small walkways to a bridge which ran across the stage at the back. These levels provided a multitude of performing spaces throughout the piece and seen alone represented a large dock which serviced ocean-going ships.

The main piece of the set is the O'Brien house which, in the original production, consisted of a large flat truck which extended the full width of the stage but, in itself was quite narrow. This truck had the ability to move up and downstage (pushed and pulled by two ASMs using boathooks). The truck was divided into three basic rooms. L was the front room-cum-bedroom, C the kitchen, R a small scullery. There was no demarcation of walls; the separate rooms being denoted by a difference of floor covering and the arrangement of furniture. The truck also had the ability to split into three, the bedroom and scullery separating from the kitchen and rolling back for the market scene.

The stackyard trucks were of a size that people could walk on them and of a scale that showed they had been unloaded from a ship. The L and R stacks lived permanently under the downstage levels L and R. This gave the actors the ability to enter straight on to the O'Brien truck. The third stackyard truck was a clever bit of design which enabled the steps of the drowning truck to be incorporated in this third stackyard truck.

The rest of the scenery was either set by hand or flown and was designed to fit in with this environment or, in the case of the Llewellyn household, to contrast with it in such a way as to create the effect in the imagination. The furniture and props should be chosen to enhance the story and any unnecessary sense of realism to overstate period will probably only get in the way, as the designer and director will realize once the pace of the show takes over. The production should feel like one continuous ribbon of action from start to finish which sweeps the audience along with it rather than allows them to sit back and watch.

The Musician

The play is not a musical and although this acting edition gives stage directions for the musician, both music and musician are optional. However, if it is decided to use a musician, it is very important that the person with this responsibility has a sensitivity and awareness of how to use music to a dramatic effect with live action as there is no place for a conductor in the piece. In the original production this man was everpresent throughout, providing a link between the scenes and often underscoring scenes to create atmosphere and tension. He was dressed in costume and sometimes remained onstage and watched the action. All instruments were real instruments and a number of them were used in conjunction with a radio mike, to achieve greater sound control. Instruments used: violin, bowed psaltery, harmonica, Jew's harp, penny whistle, hurdy-gurdy, boran, various flutes, etc.

Characters

John O'Brien Mid twenties. Over six foot and well built. With an air of responsibility beyond his years. Devoted to his family, he has never had a girlfriend in his life.

Dominic O'Brien Mid twenties. Over six foot and well built. Good looking. Arrogant, hard drinking, charming and ruthless.

Mary Ellen O'Brien Forties, looking fifties. A careworn small woman. A survivor struggling to come to terms with the demands of her family.

Shane O'Brien Fifties. Over six foot and well built. Once a hard drinking, hard fighting docker now struggling to come to terms with his physical decline.

Katie O'Brien 12–13 years. A bright, vivacious, innocent personality. A light shines from this girl that all who know her recognize.

Molly O'Brien 13–14 years. A plain, scruffy-looking child. Not too bright and full of misdirected energy.

Mick O'Brien 13–14 years. Hard kid. Leader of the kids in the street. Irresponsible and running wild.

Peter Bracken Eighties, but looks ten years younger. Intelligent and not of the same class or environment of the Fifteen Streets. There is a quiet force and dignity which emanates from this man that automatically commands respect.

Christine Bracken 18 years. A waif-like, but very determined and independent young girl. There is an intelligence and dignity which is self evident in this girl.

Hannah Kelly Forties, careworn. Stronger in physique than Mary Ellen. She is a survivor.

Joe Kelly Forties. Small, hard drinking, very aggressive docker.

Nancy Kelly 16 years. With the mind of a six year old. She is a little girl in a woman's body. She has a voice louder than necessary and a brain that works to its own rhythms. She will always be a victim.

Mary Llewellyn Twenties. Attractive, intelligent, independent and with a will of iron. She has a natural quality which enables her to move with ease between classes.

James Llewellyn Fifties, very much a self-made man. Shipyard owner but a very honest and well-respected figure in his adopted class and on the waterfront.

Beatrice Llewellyn Forties, originally of the monied classes. Her husband and daughter have been a great disappointment to her in their inability to adopt the social graces upon which her life depends.

Father O'Malley Forties. An Irish priest of the hellfire and damnation breed. Controls respect in the community through fear and knows it.

Father Bailey Fifties. An Irish priest who has lived a life before taking Holy orders. A pastoral priest whose ebullient exterior belies a shrewd and cunning intelligence which is no less effective in controlling the community than O'Malley.

Peggy Flaherty Sixties. A widower. Fat, scruffy, with heart of gold. Her gossiping and garrulous nature belies a deal of cunning.

Bella Bradley Forties. A widower. She is the hard-bitten gossip of the street. Observing and commenting on the activies of the rest of the community is her life blood.

Notes to the actors

Although the characters are real and the relationships and emotions should have a deep-rooted reality, this is a highly-stylized theatrical way of telling a story. The speed at which the story is told is vital. To get away with great emotional climaxes like the drowning of Katie one needs commitment, economy and drive and very little sentimentality. The heavy scenes should not over-indulge in tragedy. This is a rough hardened community living at a time when all they have is what they can see, but they continue to get up and keep going. The great political movements which World War I galvanized into being are only just seeds in some men's minds and there is a long way to go before the ordinary man starts getting a context in which to air his grievances. We shall live with this community for 2½ hours. We shall know them intimately by the end of this time. There is no need to overstate the obvious. The play tells a very powerful and engrossing story that will almost tell itself if given commitment and sincerity. There is a great deal more in the book than the play, and there always will be, but the power of the audience's imagination playing on a live representation should not be underestimated. What I've tried to do with this adaptation is create a powerful and engrossing piece of theatre. Something that will happen in the time it happens in and take the audience on a trip through their own emotions and imaginations. To create a piece to be involved in rather than watched and dissected. If approached in this way then the audience will go with it and love it. Your job is to read the book and then use the script to create these characters in our imaginations with strength, commitment and heart and to trust that we will add the context in which these events are to be understood.

PS. There are a great many laughs in the piece that counteract the tragedy and at first glance would seem intrusive: they are not. Be bold and stick with it, the audience need the laughs as well as the tears.

Extras
In the London production of this play, two ASMs were used to push the main O'Brien house truck back and forth onstage and set the stackyards, carry stretchers, stop fights, etc.

Doubling
Father O'Malley/Joe Kelly.
Bella Bradley/Beatrice Llewellyn.
Father Bailey/James Llewellyn.

Understudies
Played: Neighbours. Women in illness. Doctor in illness. Woman in market. Drunk in market. Butler, footman and maid in Llewellyn household. Stretcher-bearers. Men with cart. Crowd throughout.

Children
In the London production the parts of Molly and Mick were played by professional actors; the other children's parts were played by amateurs.

The Group of Kids
Two girls and eight to nine boys. They form an almost choral effect in the piece, sometimes used in a realistic way, at others to give quite a stylized effect. They are also used to set snowcloths, work in the market, etc. In a symbolic way they represent the other adult inhabitants of The Fifteen Streets; in our imaginations we credit them with the fathers, mothers, grandparents, etc., which we never see. The chants themselves are less nursery rhymes than an expression of the level of bigotry and ignorance in the community. (If the kids are singing it the parents are talking about it.) There should be nothing precious about this group; they may look like one of Sutcliffe's photographs but they are the products of a very hard environment and should be chosen and used as such.

Accents
The play is set in the North East and will only work if accents are used. However the script does not utilize a great deal of dialect and this should be avoided if the story is to be told clearly and cleanly. It is far better that the characters and story are understood than a false devotion to authenticity be employed which leaves the audience cold.

NB. In the original I deliberately picked kids with good ears and with the help of a few tapes and an authentic actor or two they can pick up the feel of the accent in much less time than an adult.

ROB BETTINSON

ACT I

SCENE 1

As the house lights go down and the CURTAIN *rises, the Musician is isolated in light in the back structure playing some kind of reel on a violin*

Shane and Dominic enter R. *They have been drinking. There is obviously a fight brewing. They are railing at each other*

Dominic Who do you think you are calling me like that?
Shane I'm your bloody father . . .
Dominic I never asked to be set on the ore boat. You don't own the docks, Da!

He exits L

(*Off*) It's not my fault you're past it.
Shane (*taking his jacket off*) Past it, am I. Why you . . . (*He throws his jacket off* L) I'll show you who's bloody past it. Here, get some of this, you long skinny streak . . .

He goes off L. *There is a slap off, then a loud groan from Shane. He backs onstage holding his face; followed by Dominic*

Dominic (*as he enters*) Too slow, Da. Too slow.

He exits L

Shane (*following*) Get here! I'll show you who's past it.

He exits L

The Lights change

SCENE 2

Hannah Kelly is in a pool of light DR *possing her washing*

The group of kids run on shouting "Fight! Fight!", etc., and form up DL *as if looking through the O'Briens' front window. They continue with controlled enthusiasm until Mary Ellen enters*

Bella Bradley is on a level above Hannah DR. *To call Hannah's attention she bangs with her heel on the floor. Peggy Flaherty is on a level* DL. *Father Bailey is in the back structure* R, *watching. Father O'Malley is in the back structure* L, *watching. Other females if available in the back structure* C

All the above happens at the same time and the lighting isolates all these groups separately

Kids Fight! Fight! Fight! The O'Briens are fighting! . . . *etc.*
Bella Hannah! Hannah! Get yourself up here quick! The O'Briens are at it
    again—blue murder!
Peggy Holy Mary, not again. (*Shouting through the floor*) Can a body get
    no peace! Stop it, the both of you!
Hannah (*shouting up*) Stop your bloody racket!
Peggy (*to the kids*) Stop your shouting! You blood-thirsty hooligans!
Hannah Stop your banging or you'll have the plaster down.
Peggy (*banging on the floor*) See sense, you idiots! Can there be no peace
    between you!
Hannah (*throwing her washing down*) God curse you! Bella bloody flabby-
    gob! (*She goes up*)
Peggy (*to the kids*) Stop your shouting or you'll have the polis down on us.
Hannah (*going to Bella*) Stop your banging, will you woman! Our Joe
    warned me I'd never have a moment's peace once you moved in! (*She sees
    the fight*) Oh my God . . .
Peggy And I'll have less of your cheek, Annie Kelly, or I'll be over there to
    see your ma.

The kids jeer Annie Kelly

Kids (*chanting*) The O'Briens are fighting.
               The air's all blood and snot,
               The fight'll go on all the night
               Till someone gets the chop!

Peggy goes off

Bella It's the old windbag and Dominic!
Hannah Who else could it be?
Bella Drunk as lords the both of them.

Peggy appears with a potty and threatens the kids

Peggy So help me, I'll give yer mas something to leather you for . . . (*She is
    about to throw the potty*)

*A po crashes through a window underneath her and smashes on to the stage.
The kids go quiet*

Hannah Eeh! My God, Bella! He's thrown the pot through the window!
    That'll bring the polis.
Bella Serve 'em right, drunken idiots!

Mary Ellen enters

Hannah There's Mary Ellen . . .

*All goes quiet. Mary Ellen walks to the centre and retrieves the broken pieces
of pot. She does not acknowledge the onlookers*

Peggy (*to Mary Ellen*) Are you all right, lass?
Hannah Eeh! It's enough to bring on her bairn.
Bella Who wants a bairn at forty-five, I ask you. She should have been more

cute. I could have got her something would've skited all the troubles out
of her.

Hannah She's a Catholic, Bella!

Bella Catholic, be damned! They tell them to have bairns but do they
bloody well keep them?

Hannah Poor lass . . . she looks like death.

Bella, Peggy and Hannah are shaking their heads in sympathy

Mary Ellen leaves the stage

The kids creep behind her

Peggy Haven't you got homes to go to? Go on, bugger off and play in your
own yards, pestering the life out of the poor soul. Go on, away with you
. . . (*She threatens them with the slops*)

The kids jeer and run off

The Lights isolate Bella and Hannah

Hannah Pity John hadn't have been there. He'd soon have put a stop to
them two all right.

Bella Ay, that Shane and Dominic, they're both alike, full of wind and
water. By God, if I was in Mary Ellen's place for five minutes, I'd soon lay
those two boozy sods flat with the poker. She's soft her, soft as clarts . . .

The O'Brien truck rolls forward. Hannah starts to go

Bella You won't forget to knock up if you hear owt like.

Hannah Ay, I will.

Bella (*shouting down to her*) You wait till next Thursday week, eh? When
Dominic's wearing his shamrock. There'll be skull and hair flying around
then all right. The fifteen streets won't hold him. You won't forget to
knock up now, will you?

Hannah (*now below*) God give me peace! Bella bloody Bradley!

She picks up her tub and goes

SCENE 3

*As the above scene ends, the O'Briens' truck rolls forward. The central area is
the main kitchen-cum-parlour. R the scullery. L the front room-cum-bedroom*

*Mary Ellen is in the front room, righting furniture. Shane and Dominic are in
the kitchen, glaring at each other. Katie and Molly are also there at the back
keeping a very low profile*

*As the Lights come up, the kids cross the stage through the structure at the
back. They are playing a game and chanting a song they have made up*

Kids   The O'Briens are fighting.
             One of them is dead.
             His da hit him with an axe
             And chopped off his head.

During the above, Mary Ellen has righted the furniture. She picks up a broken picture frame, takes the picture, folds it, snaps the frame apart in frustration, walks to the scullery. She throws the pieces in a box containing firewood, puts the picture somewhere safe and returns to the kitchen

Mary Ellen (*to Shane*) Satisfied, are you, now?
Dominic (*laughing*) Oh, ey, having a go at Da, are you?
Shane Why you ... (*He is about to go for Dominic*)
Mary Ellen You! Get yourself to bed.
Dominic (*laughing*) All right, old girl. But you——
Mary Ellen Bed!

He laughs and goes to the front room, sits on the bed. Mary Ellen follows. During the following she undresses him and puts him to bed

Dominic If he wasn't my old man, I'd have knocked him stiff. But I'll break his bloody neck next time he messes with me. I didn't ask to be set on the bloody ore boat for Christ's sake! They want the young 'uns down the holds. It's not my fault he's past it!
Mary Ellen Shut it!
Dominic (*laughing*) Well, for some things, anyway.

She pushes him back on the bed in anger

All right, Ma, sorry.
Mary Ellen Mind your filthy tongue!
Dominic The way he carries on he'll be lucky if any of the gaffers'll start him.
Mary Ellen He had two shifts this week.
Dominic Ay, and you know as well as I do it nearly bloody killed him. That's all he's fit for now, the old sod. (*Nearly asleep*) You tell him. He tries it on with me again, it'll be the last time. I'll bury him. Who the hell does he think he is ... calling me like that ... the old sod ...

Mary Ellen finishes undressing him, takes his wages out of his trouser pocket, divides this in two, replaces some, puts the rest in a little cloth bag pinned on the underside of her apron. She re-enters the kitchen. Shane is dozing. There is a little self-conscious cough off R

Mary Ellen (*staying in the kitchen*) Yes, Peggy, what is it you want?
Peggy (*off*) I was warming meself up with a mouthful of stew, Mary Ellen, and I said to meself, "I'll take a drop below, it'll stick to Mary Ellen's ribs."
Mary Ellen (*to herself*) Ay, if it doesn't kill us first. Well Peggy, you'd better come in.

Peggy enters quickly

Peggy Are you all right, lass?
Mary Ellen Yes, I'm all right, Peggy. Thanks for the soup.
Peggy You'll drink it now, won't you, Mary Ellen?
Mary Ellen Yes, yes.
Peggy It's for yourself, mind, don't go giving it to the others.

Mary Ellen I wouldn't dream of it.

Molly sniggers, Katie shuts her up

Now, was there . . . ?

Peggy (*loudly for Shane's benefit*) Do the bairn that's coming a power of good, that will, I promise you . . .

Mary Ellen (*sighing*) Ay . . .

Peggy Eeeh, Mary Ellen . . . God and His Holy Mother preserve us this day, the trials we have! (*She pauses*) Is there anything more I can do for you, Mary Ellen?

Mary Ellen I'm all right, Peggy, thanks.

Peggy (*leaning to speak to Mary Ellen*) Did I ever tell you, Mary Ellen, the late Mr Flaherty's cure for all this?

Mary Ellen No, Peggy.

Peggy Iducation! No man would fight, he said, once he had iducation. And he knew what he was talking about, for he got about among the gentry, my Charlie, you know . . .

Mary Ellen Are you sure you haven't left yourself short, Peggy?

Peggy Not at all. Not at all. Now you sit yourself down and don't talk any more. I'll be away upstairs now. And make sure you get that down you, it'll put a lining on your stomach. Now, you two girls, stop your playing and help your ma. And remember, Mary Ellen, if you want any advice, you know where to come.

She goes

Mary Ellen Katie? Here, and for God's sake don't let her see you.

Katie goes off with the stew

Molly Aw, Mam, can I have some? I'm starving.

Mary Ellen (*clipping her*) Stop whining and wait for your tea! Hell would have to have frozen over before I'd let any of you eat her potions.

Katie enters followed by Mick

Katie Done it. Here's the bowl.

Mary Ellen Good girl. Now wash your hands.

Mick Ma, why was our Katie pouring food down the grate?

Mary Ellen (*clipping him*) Mind your own business!

Molly (*to Mick*) Hell would have had to have frozen over before you can eat one of her potions!

Mick Eh?

Mary Ellen Right, that's enough from you two. I don't want the whole of the fifteen streets knowing our business. Understand? Mick?

He nods

And especially not her upstairs.

They both nod

Good. Here, this'll keep you quiet.

She puts three plates of bread and dripping on the table. They begin to eat

John enters. He takes his jacket off in the scullery and washes

Mary Ellen puts John's tea on the table

Mick Got anything, John? Any bananas or anything?

John Not the night. We're still on the grain boat.

Mick What about the morrer? What's come in the day? Will you get us a banana the morrer? Will you? You haven't given us a banana in ages!

Mary Ellen Get on with your bread and dripping.

John sits at the table. Mary Ellen puts another plate out

(*To Shane*) Your tea's out.

Shane (*resentful*) Served last now, am I?

Mary Ellen What? I ... I've just put it on the table ...

Shane It's a difference when you're not bringing it in.

Mary Ellen Sit down ...

Shane You've got to work or you don't eat ... least not till every bugger else is finished.

John I'll wait till you're done. (*He stares at Shane*)

Shane (*cutting away from John's gaze*) It's them young 'uns—I was never set on before me father.

Mary Ellen (*quietly*) Don't be a fool ... get your tea.

Shane (*exploding at Mary Ellen*) You starting, are you? That's all it needs, for you to start belittling me before the bairns.

John Da! (*He makes to get up*)

Mary Ellen No, John ...

Shane Oh, ay. I see ... the next bloody thing'll be there's the bloody door, get out! (*He storms out of the back door and kicks a bucket of water over as he goes*) I'm sick of it ... Sick to death of this bloody dump ...

He goes off

Mary Ellen follows him to the scullery

Mary Ellen Shane! Sh——(*She looks down at the water*) God give me strength! (*To herself*) Shane O'Brien, you haven't the brains you were born with! (*She wipes a tear, touches her belly. She starts clearing up the mess*)

Katie I'll help you, Ma.

Mary Ellen No! Get up out of that. That's the only clean pinny you've got!

Katie Well, I haven't got to go to school the morrer.

Mary Ellen Doesn't matter. Get up out of that.

John (*crossing to her*) Here! Let's have it.

Mary Ellen Oh, get out of me road, the both of you!

They return to the kitchen. Mary Ellen mops up the mess. She is very tired. She returns to the kitchen

Mick, go and empty the bucket and wash it out and bring some clean water. See you wash it out, mind!

Mick Aw! Why can't she do it? (*He digs Molly in the ribs*)
Molly Look at him, Ma! Stop it, our Mick!
John Your mother spoke to you.
Mick Me ear's bad. It's been running all day.
John You going out to play the night?
Mick Why, ay!
John Then empty the bucket.

Mick does so reluctantly

Molly sniggers

Mary Ellen You'll laugh the other side of your face in a minute, my girl. Get those dishes washed.
Molly Then can I go out and play?
Mary Ellen You're not going to run the streets?
Molly We're going in Annie Kelly's wash-house. Her ma's had the pot on and it's warm, and we're going to play houses and dress up.
Mary Ellen Well, only half an hour, mind. And you can take Katie with you.
Katie I don't want to go, Ma. I've got to do some homework.
Mary Ellen What?
John You got your sums wrong?
Katie (*smiling*) No.
John Then why do you have to do homework?
Katie I've got to learn something. Miss Llewellyn asked me to ...
Molly She's Miss Llewellyn's pet, everybody says she is ...
Katie No I'm not!
Molly I hated Miss Llewellyn. I was glad when I got moved up.
John I should imagine she was pretty pleased an' all! I think you must be the cleverest lass in all the school.
Katie That's what Miss Llewellyn says! She's says I'm advanced and I must work nights and ... and read a lot.
John Well, there you are, then.

Molly bangs the plates down, goes out, turns in the scullery

Molly   Miss Llewellyn has a swellin'
                An' I'm not tellin'
                Where Miss Llewellyn
                Has a swellin'.

Molly exits

John and Mary Ellen burst out laughing

Katie Oh, our John, you're laughing! Our Molly's awful. Miss Llewellyn hasn't got a ... she's lovely, she's beautiful ...
John Here we go again, Ma.
Katie She is, our John. She wears a lovely white blouse with a frill at the neck and her hair's brown and shines all over the place.
John We know, and she doesn't walk, she floats on air.

Katie John, stop it. She's lovely.

John Even when she gives you the stick?

Katie She doesn't ever!

John Get away, I bet our Molly and Mick'd have something to say on that subject, eh, Ma?

Mary Ellen Ay.

Katie She's wonderful.

John We know. You keep telling us. She walks like a princess and talks like a queen and all the men from far around think she's the prettiest woman they've ever seen.

Katie Mr Culbert's after her! Cathleen Pearson says he wants to marry her.

John (*laughing hysterically*) Lucky Mr Culbert! Is that his real name?

Katie Yes, Mr Gilbert Culbert.

John Oooh! Did you hear that, Ma? Mr Gilbert Culbert. And who's he when he's out?

Katie He's a teacher at St Jude's.

John He'd have to be with a name like that.

Katie Oh, our John, you're awful. (*She scrambles up on him*)

John Here, hold on!

Katie Eeeeh! You haven't got to say that.

John What? "Hold on"?

Katie Yes. Miss Llewellyn says you've got to say "Wait a moment" or "Stop a moment".

John Do you hear that, Ma ... Miss Llewellyn says we don't talk proper, like. Maybe I should go back to school. It'd beat working in the docks that's for sure. Mind you, I don't fancy the sound of this Mr Culbert Gilbert or whatever his name is. Well, young lady, what is it you've to learn the night?

Katie I already know some of it. A man called Shakespeare did it.

John Haway then!

She gets off his knee and stands. She recites

Katie   "There take an inventory of all I have,
               To the last penny; 'tis the king's; my role
               And my integrity to heaven is all I dare call
               My own. O Cr——" (*She stops*)

Dominic has entered from the bedroom, somewhat hungover. He smiles, claps slowly

Dominic Where's me tea?

Mary Ellen Get yourself dressed first. You're not sitting at my table in that state.

Dominic No. (*He goes to sit*)

John (*rising; angrily*) Get dressed!

They are ready to fight

Mary Ellen No John ... please! No more the day!

Dominic breaks off

Dominic (*to John*) Yes, teacher. (*He returns to the bedroom to dress*)
John Go on. It's all right ...
Katie   "O Cromwell, Cromwell!
        Had I but serv'd my God with half the zeal
        I serv'd my king——"

Molly enters

Molly (*shouting*) Ma! Ma! Do you know what?
Mary Ellen Make less noise!
Molly But, Ma, there's somebody moving in next door the morrer.
Mary Ellen Wash yourself and get ready for bed ...
Molly Aw, Ma. That's not fair ... I only came back to tell you ...
Mary Ellen Now!
Molly Aw.
Mary Ellen Finish it, pet.
Katie   "Had I but serv'd my God with half the zeal
        I serv'd my king, he would not in my age
        Have left me naked to mine enemies."

Mary Ellen wipes a tear

John (*sweeping Katie into his arms*) Will I push you through to Mrs Flaherty?
Katie Eeeh! No, John! Eeeeh, our John, let me down.
Molly There's someone moving in next door the morrer, John!
John You'll soon be cleverer than Mrs Flaherty then people will come round here asking for advice. And you'll say——

Dominic enters

Molly Dominic, there's someone moving in next door the morrer!
Mary Ellen Who told you this?
Molly Mrs Bradley told Annie Kelly's ma, and Annie Kelly told me.
Dominic Ay, well, Bella flabbygob'll know right enough. Go and ask her what time they're coming.

Molly makes to go

Mary Ellen Stupid, big lass. He's only fooling you. (*To Dominic*) There's your tea! (*To Molly*) Now, get undressed.
Molly Aww!
Mary Ellen Now!
Molly Aw, Ma!

The Lights change

SCENE 4

Music. The O'Brien truck rolls half-way US

Bella (*hammering on the floor with her heel*) Hannah! Hannah! Come on up quick and see the state of this! They're here, and a bloody great van an' all.

Hannah enters to Bella

The Lights come up on the Brackens and the O'Briens. The Brackens, Peter, Christine and David, have various hand luggage and form a picture DSL. *The O'Briens form a picture looking out at their new neighbours. A light comes up on Peggy Flaherty watching. The rest of the kids form another picture, a tight group hanging in the back structure. Fathers Bailey and O'Malley also watch*

Hannah Eeh! Well, I never . . . have they got the right street, d'ye think?
Bella He's not married to that lass, is he?
Hannah No, Bella! That's scandalous. He's old enough to be her granda' for heaven's sake!
Bella Why else would the likes of them be coming to the fifteen streets? Look at the furniture, and in a van an' all.
Hannah Carpets an' all. They'll be lucky to get half of that in.

Peter Bracken exits L

Bella That'll be their bairn.
Hannah Eeeh, no. She's not old enough . . .
Bella I'm telling you why else. Hiding, that's what they are.
Hannah No, he's ten years old if a day . . .
Bella Eeeh, God, butter wouldn't melt . . . the hooligans round here'll make mincemeat out of the little bugger.
Hannah She's a bit skinny, isn't she?
Bella Ay, nowt on her for a dog to eat.
Hannah She's like a lad.
Bella Well, there's one doesn't think so.

Dominic has crossed to Christine and offers to carry her bag. They turn with him and go

The Lights go down on the O'Briens and Brackens, leaving Hannah and Bella

Hannah Well, there's one O'Brien with a foot in the door.
Bella Ay, there's no flies on him all right! Fancy the like of those toffs moving next door to the fighting O'Briens!
Hannah Ay, I hope they don't expect to sleep nights!
Bella There's a skeleton or two rattling around in those fancy wardrobes, I'll be bound.
Hannah D'ye think?
Bella Ay, why else? Nowt good'll come of this, I'm telling ye. Come on, let's get a closer look.
Hannah No, Bella.
Bella Come on. You'll not get another chance to see such stuff, for you can guarantee they won't be asking the likes of you and me round to dinner. Come on!

She drags her off

The Lights change

The O'Briens' house. Mary Ellen, John and Shane are in the front bedroom looking off L as if out of the front window. As the Lights come up Shane breaks for the kitchen

Shane Must be millionaires, those buggers. Know who they are?
Mary Ellen No. I know nowt about them. What are they doing down here?
Nancy (*off*) Can I come in, Mrs O'Brien?
Shane (*to Mary Ellen*) No!
Mary Ellen Oh, it's you, Nancy. Yes, come on in.

Nancy Kelly enters. She is a girl of sixteen. She has the mind of an eight-year-old. She looks a bit simple, yet she tries to be grown-up. John is the most relaxed with her

Nancy (*formally*) Hello, Mrs O'Brien.
Mary Ellen (*playing the ritual greeting for Nancy's sake*) Hello, Nancy.
Nancy Hello, John.
John Hello there, Nancy.
Nancy Hello, Mr O'Brien.

Shane mutters something but does not look at her

    Hello, Mr O'Brien.
Shane (*still not looking; tensely*) Hello.
Mary Ellen Sit yourself down, Nancy. We haven't seen you since the summer. You look well.
Nancy Thank you Mrs O'Brien.(*Pause*)There's people moving in next dooɪ
Shane Never!
John Yes, there are, Nancy. Still like your place, Nancy?
Nancy Yes, John. I've been there nearly a month now.
Shane (*to John*) She's a bloody imbecile, man!
John Yes, you have, Nancy.
Mary Ellen (*gently*) It's four years nearly.
Nancy (*puzzled*) Maybe?
John You look very nice the day, Nancy.
Nancy (*brightening immediately*) This is a new coat. Me ma bought it. And these boots an' all. And I've got a silk dress with a sash. And I'm going to get a hat with a feather in.

Shane noisily scrapes back his chair and goes out

    Is Mr O'Brien in a bad mood?
Mary Ellen No, love, it's just his dinner didn't agree with him.
Nancy Oh, he's not ill again, is he?

Mary Ellen and John both laugh at this

John Don't worry yourself, Nancy. It's nothing he can't live with.

Dominic enters from the front. He sees Nancy and greets her, mimicking her greeting

Dominic Hel-lo, Nancy.

Nancy Hello, Dominic.

Dominic What's this I'm hearing about you, Nancy? They tell me you're courtin'.

Nancy Eeh! Who told you that? Eeh! I'm not ... am I, John?

John (*irritated by Dominic's manner*) No, pet!

Dominic Well, that's what I heard. I thought you were going to wait for me. Nice one, you are.

Nancy Eeh! Dominic! I haven't got a lad, I haven't. I don't let them come near me. If they touch me, I yells. I do. (*She is upset by his teasing*)

John Knock it off ...

Dominic Let's get this settled. When are me and you goin' out for a walk, eh?

Mary Ellen (*interrupting*) I think you'd better be going home now, Nancy. Your ma will be wondering where you are.

Nancy makes to go

Dominic I'll get another lass, mind.

Mary Ellen That's enough of that! Get away home, now, Nancy!

Hannah Kelly enters

Hannah Oh, this is where you are. I guessed as much. Go on, get yourself over home. Now!

Nancy obediently goes

Well, what d'ye think eh? D'ye know who you've got next door, Mary Ellen? My God!

Mary Ellen What are they?

Hannah Spooks!

Mary Ellen What?

Hannah Spooks. He's called the Spook of Jarrow and Howden and round there. Remember a bit back when the Irish navvies burnt a hut down and the polis had to get the man away? Well, that was him. He was givin' a service or something. Dorrie Clark knew who he was the minute she set eyes on him and she was tellin' Bella Bradley that when she was delivering once in Jarrow he came in and wanted to lay his hands on the woman. That's what she said ... lay his hands on her! Did you ever hear owt like it? To ease her labour, he said, because she'd been in it four days.

Mary Ellen (*shocked*) Did she let him?

Hannah Did she hell! Ye know old Dorrie. She said she kicked his arse out of the door. And she would an' all, full of gin or not. But, by God, there'll be the devil's figarties around these doors before long! Mark my words. Ye'll see.

Mary Ellen (*disturbed by this*) What d'ye make of it, John?

John (*getting up and moving to the front room for his coat*) I don't know. They looked all right to me.

Hannah Mind yerself, John lad, that she don't lay hands on you. They say the lass is as bad as the old man. (*To Dominic*) And you, there, you've soon got your leg in.

Dominic Do you know what the old man works at?
Hannah Now that's another funny thing. He's the Mr Bracken that has the boot shop in Jarrow.

All are surprised

Dominic Boot shop, eh? Well, I'll be ...

John starts to leave

Mary Ellen Going for a walk, lad?
John Ay, where's Katie?
Mary Ellen Out the back. Make sure she has a wash first. I don't want her seen in that state!

Dominic stops Mary Ellen in the scullery and whispers

Dominic Any chance of you lending me the money to get me clothes out the pawn?
Mary Ellen They've been there the month.
Dominic Well, I want them now.
Mary Ellen I've only got the rent. You put your suit in. You'll have to get it out.
Dominic I'll give it you back next week.
Mary Ellen I haven't got it. I've only got a few coppers for the gas over the weekend.

Dominic sulkily retreats to the front room and throws himself on the bed

Hannah Your lad'll be after chasing that girl next door.
Mary Ellen Who?
Hannah Who else? (*She gestures to the front room*)
Mary Ellen Well, more fool him. As long as she leaves our John alone, that's all I care. Now, tell me, what else did Bella say about the spooks ... ?

The Lights change and the O'Briens' house moves back

SCENE 6

A lone Musican high in the back structure plays harmonica

Katie and John enter. They are in the country

John I've seen the ships, Katie. I spent every day last week in them. Morning till night. I come up here to forget them, not to sit up here admiring them all day.
Katie They are beautiful, but aren't they?
John Ay. They're more than beautiful. One day you'll understand, then you'll run up here of a Saturday as fast as your legs'll carry you.
Katie I like coming up here, John.
John Ay, look up there. Those clouds. They look like a fleet of white brakes off for a day's outing, don't they?
Katie Where ...

John There!

Katie Oh they do. They really do.

John I bet they're off to the country too. Morpeth or some place.

Katie And I bet when they come back they'll be singing. Like the people do on the brake trips. (*She sings*) A'am back to canny auld Jarrer.

Father Bailey enters

Father Bailey (*singing*) A hip, a hip hooray!

Katie Father Bailey!

Father Bailey Hello, there, Katie! John, nice day to be out. Out for a walk, the pair of you?

Katie Yes, Father. We always come up here for a walk, Saturdays.

Father Bailey Just the day for it. You know, John, I believe you get taller.

John It's the clothes, Father, they've shrunk.

Father Bailey And now, Katie O'Brien, what honours have you been gathering on your head this week? Do you know we have a clever girl here, John? Every week I hear something about Katie O'Brien. She's top of her class for this, that and the other. It'll be teaching the teachers she'll be doing in the end.

John Ay, maybe.

Father Bailey Everything all right with you, John?

John Yes, Father.

Father Bailey And your new neighbours?

John News travels fast.

Father Bailey (*laughing*) Ay, and you'd be surprised how fast. Well?

John They seem all right to me.

Father Bailey Ay, well, we'll see. I'm just on me way down to the fifteen streets. I'll look in on your mother. How is she?

John Just middling, Father.

Father Bailey And your da, and Dominic?

John Things don't change.

Father Bailey Oh, you're wrong there, John. Every minute of the day they're changing.

John Ay. Well, I hadn't noticed it.

Father Bailey Will I be seeing you at Mass tomorrow?

John I don't think so, Father.

Father Bailey Oh, this'll never do. Not at all. I'll have to come and have a crack with you soon. Or should I ask Father O'Malley to pay you a visit?

John I don't think so somehow, Father.

Father Bailey (*smiling*) No, well, maybe not. But I must be off now. Enjoy your walk, the both of you. Goodbye.

John
Katie } (*together*) Goodbye.

Father Bailey exits

Katie He won't send Father O'Malley round, will he?

John No.

Katie Good. He scares me.

John Well, that's you and half the fifteen streets, bonny lass. (*He sits*)

Katie I will be a teacher one day, won't I, John?

John I thought we'd agreed we'd leave Miss Llewellyn and school and Mr Whatsisname to amuse themselves for the day.

Katie Sorry ... it's just ...

John Go on, what?

Katie You do want me to be a teacher, don't you, John?

John Oh, lass ... Katie ... of course I do ...

Katie Miss Llewellyn says I can be if I——

John There you go again. Miss Llewellyn says this. Miss Llewellyn says that ... give it a rest, will you? It's very easy for your Miss Llewellyn to say you're going to be a teacher but it's just not that easy ...

Katie If I work hard, John. She says I've got to work hard.

John I know that, bonny lass, but sometimes it doesn't matter how hard you work. How hard you want something. Things just don't turn out like you want.

Katie Why not?

John Oh, pet. If I knew the answer to that do you think we'd still be living where we are? Eh? (*After a pause*) I don't know the answer, Katie. And if I did, you wouldn't like it. You'll understand when you get older.

Katie (*upset*) But I want to be a teacher. It's what I want. Miss Llewellyn says I could be. She says ... I want to be a teacher, John.

John (*holding her to him*) Ay, and you might be one day, pet. You might. There's just nowt I can do about it. It's the Miss Llewellyns you'll have to ask about it, not me. I just don't know how, that's all. If it was up to me, I'd build you a school myself. Here, in these fields, with the birds and the trees. "Katie O'Brien's School." Now how would that suit you?

Katie Don't be daft, our John. Who'd come to it? No-one lives up here.

John (*laughing*) You could teach the rabbits. You'd get more sense out of them than half the lot in the fifteen streets.

Katie Don't be daft, our John!

John That's it. Smile, and keep smiling. Now, promise, no more Miss Llewellyn and I'll finish the story as we walk up to the Robin Hood.

Katie Oh, yes. Yes, please, John.

John Now, where had we got to?

Katie The dance, the dance. She was all dressed up by her Fairy Godmother and wondering how she was going to get there and ... and ... (*She starts tugging at John's sleeve. She sees Miss Llewellyn off*)

John Well, the next part is really——What is it?

Katie (*whispering*) It's her.

John What?

Katie There ... it's her.

John Who?

Miss Llewellyn enters

Katie You know.

John No, I don't. Who is it, Katie?
Katie (*whispering in his ear*) Miss Llewellyn.
John Gerraway!
Katie It is! It is!
John (*flabbergasted*) That's ... ?

Katie nods and is smiling at Miss Llewellyn who has crossed to them

Mary Hello, Katie.
Katie Hello, Miss Llewellyn.
Mary You're a long way from home.
Katie Yes, Miss Llewellyn.
Mary (*smiling at John*) You're John, aren't you?
John (*embarrassed*) Yes, ma'am.
Mary I knew you were. Katie often tells me about your walks. I've heard
such a lot about you.

He tries to smile

I don't suppose you know, but you are a combination of Prince Charming
and God to a certain young lady.
John Neither of them would be flattered. And if the last one hears of it,
there's not much chance of me getting up there.

She laughs. He joins in. Katie enjoys them laughing together

Mary I don't suppose that will worry you very much. I should take the
heaven you're sure of. (*After a pause*) Well, I'll see you on Monday
morning, Katie. I'm glad to have met you in the flesh, for now when I
listen to your sayings being recorded I'll be able to place them. Goodbye.
Goodbye, Katie.

She goes

Katie Goodbye, Miss Llewellyn.
John Goodbye.

They watch her go

You don't tell her all I say, do you?
Katie (*lying*) Oh, no! Isn't she lovely?
John Yes ... yes, she is. She's beautiful, all right.
Katie (*looking to John and at the docks, then, beaming*) And isn't it a lovely
day!
John (*laughing*) Ay, it's a lovely day. A day of clean wind and far mastheads
and bonnie lasses.
Katie Oh, John, that was like poetry.
John (*laughing and going*) Ay, well, don't you go telling that one to your
Miss Llewellyn.
Katie (*lying*) Oh, no, John, I told you, I don't.
John And you never told me she looked like that, either.

They exit

Katie (*off*) Oh, our John, I did. I did tell you. You know I did.

The Lights change

SCENE 7

The Musician enters playing the Jew's harp (miked)

At the same instant the Protestants enter in the back structure UL, *the Catholics from* L *to* DR *at stage level. The Protestants have blue ribbons about their persons, the Catholics green*

Protestants   Catholic, Catholic, ring the bell,
                     When you die, you'll go to hell!
Catholics   Protestant, Protestant, you dirty lot,
                     Yer backside's blue and yer nose all snot!

David Bracken enters and watches

Protestants   Catholic, Catholic, ring the bell,
                     When you die, you'll go to hell!
Mick (*seeing David Bracken*) Look, there's the Spook!
All Where? Look there's the Spook! Spooky!

They all surround David Bracken, pushing and taunting him

You're the Spook! You're the Spook, You're the Spook! Spook! Spook!
Spook! Spook! Spook! . . . (*And on until they can't do it any faster*)
Mick (*grabbing David and pushing the others off him*) Let him away!

A big lad challenges Mick; Mick throws him back into the group

Come on, Spooky, we'll give you ten start!
Others (*cheering then chanting*) To the gut! To the gut! To the gut! . . .
Mick Ten start! Ready . . . (*He thumps David*) Ready?
Others (*chanting*) Run! Run! Run! . . .
Mick (*pushing David*) Run!

David breaks for the back structure R. *All cheer. At the same time Mick signals and two lads break for the back structure* L *to cut him off*

All One! Two! Three! Four! (*Very fast the rest*) Five! Six! Seven! Eight nine
ten!

All cheer and run after David

David runs L *in the back structure, sees the other lads cutting off his exit. He stops, runs off* R

The rest of the kids follow, cheering

Molly is about to follow when . . .

Mary Ellen emerges from R *wing and drags her off*

The Lights change

SCENE 8

John enters R, *carrying David Bracken, Christine in attendance. They cross and go off*

As they cross the O'Brien truck rolls forward, the Lights come up and the music stops

Mary Ellen enters through the scullery dragging Molly

Mary Ellen (*cracking Molly round the head*) I'll gut you! A big lass like you running mad with a lot of lads! Now get over there and not a peep out of you!

John enters through the front followed by Christine

Christine John! Wait, please.
John Hadn't you better stay by the lad?
Christine Please, John. Don't thrash him. You'll only make it worse. You'll only thrash it into him.
John Look we've been through all this. The last thing on this earth I'm going to do is sit down and talk to him. This is the fifteen streets you're living in. Not the best part of Jarrow or Howden or whatever you're used to, and you'd better get used to that idea pretty fast. For your own sakes. Now, if you don't mind, I'll deal with him as I see fit. Now, hadn't you better get back to the lad?

Christine goes

(*Entering the kitchen*) Where is he?
Mary Ellen Is the lad all right?
John Just. (*He shouts*) Mick! Get here, now! (*He starts to take his belt off*)
Mick (*off* R) I'm not coming! I'll tell me da.
John Get here!
Mary Ellen Go canny, lad.

During the following, Mick enters sheepishly

John (*sharply*) Go canny? Now don't you start. He's nearly killed the lad. As it is, he's nearly sent him out of his mind. I found the little bugger hitting him with a stick, trying to push him into the water. In the river. In the gut!

She looks at Mick

He would have an' all. He was laughing, enjoying it, the little ... if you hadn't got hold of our Molly when you did, you'd have more than a good thrashing on your plate, the night. Mick!

Mick breaks for the front door. John grabs him

Mary Ellen John, easy ...
Mick Ma, Ma, don't let him!

John starts to drag him off out the back

Dominic enters

Dominic What you at? Playing boss of the house again?

John You mind your own damn business! If you'd had a little more of it, there might have been an improvement in you! Step aside!

Mary Ellen He's nearly killed the lad next door.

Dominic steps aside

John drags Mick off

Throughout the rest, Dominic quickly tidies himself up

Your tea's in the oven. I'll get it.

Dominic I don't want that yet.

Mary Ellen Where are you going?

Dominic (*smiling*) Where d'ye think? To console our neighbours in their hour of need.

He goes out the front, whistling

Mary Ellen (*shouting*) No whistling!

He doesn't stop. The Lights close, isolating Mary Ellen

Sweet Lady of our Lord, bless us and protect us from the evil next door. (*She crosses herself as . . .*)

The Lights fade

Scene 9

The lone fiddler plays. Katie is in the house. Shane is in. Dominic is in the toilet, off. John is repairing Katie's boots. Mary Ellen is irritated and finishing making the bed in the front bedroom

Dominic enters from the backyard, jacket over his head, flies undone

Shane Still bad?

Dominic Cats and bloody dogs! If it keeps this up, there'll be no work the morrer either.

Mary Ellen Then get down on your knees and pray for a break for I couldn't stand another day with you all for company.

John If it eases off, I'll get Katie out of your way. Would you like to go for a walk later, Katie?

Katie How can I without me shoes? Have you finished them yet?

John No, not quite.

Katie I've got to go to school the morrer. I can't stay off another day 'cos of me shoes. Can I, Ma?

Mary Ellen Get out of me way, girl! You should be grateful John's mending them for you or you'd be missing the week.

Katie starts crying

Now don't start that again or I'll send you to bed.

There is a knock on the back door

I'm warning you, madam. Now go and make yourself useful and answer
the door.

Katie goes

God save me, if she so much as mentions that Miss Llewellyn's name
again, I'll be in the madhouse. (*She is looking to the back door*) Heaven
help us! I'm not having them in here! (*She goes out to the scullery*)

Katie brings into the scullery Peter and Christine Bracken

Hold on, Katie, I'll see to it.

Peter Good-afternoon, Mrs O'Brien. I thought we'd just come round and
get acquainted. And also to ask you to thank your son for helping my boy
last night.

Mary Ellen (*curtly*) That's all right. It was our Mick's fault anyway.

John (*moving Mary Ellen to one side*) Won't you come in?

Peter Thank you. Thank you. Are you by any chance the Mr O'Brien we
owe so much to?

John (*placing two chairs*) Take a seat. It is us should be doing the thanking.
Not many people would be taking it like this. This is my father.

Peter (*taking Shane's hand and shaking it*) My name's Peter Bracken and
this is my granddaughter, Christine.

Shane (*standing and making his way to the scullery*) Ay, well I'm just off to
see if there's anything come in. (*He grabs his coat in the scullery. To Mary
Ellen as he goes*) Get them out of my bloody house, now!

Shane goes

Mary Ellen But . . . (*To herself*) Shane.

An awkward silence

John (*to Christine*) Won't you sit down, please.

Christine (*sitting*) Hello. I'm Christine.

Katie Katie.

Christine And what's this book you're reading?

Katie *Hansel and Gretel* by the Brothers Grimm. I know it by heart. Our
John got it for me.

Christine Do you like books?

Katie At school I do. Miss . . . my teacher sometimes lets me bring them
home. But this is mine.

Christine Well, you must come next door sometime. David's got some I'm
sure he's finished with. Would you like that?

Katie Oh, yes please. I'd've been at school today only me boots were
lea——

Mary Ellen Katie, haven't you got any homework to be getting on with?

Katie No!

An awkward pause

Peter I suppose you must be kept busy, Mrs O'Brien?

Mary Ellen (*forcing herself to look at Peter*) Yes, most of the time I'm at it.
Peter You must find it very hard looking after such a big family. And I
    mean big. (*He laughs*)
Mary Ellen Well, you've got to take what God sends. I mean . . .

John and Dominic stare at Mary Ellen

Peter (*laughing*) Well, he certainly sent you a houseful.

Mary Ellen smiles. There is a knock at the front door

> *Katie goes to answer*

Christine Will you let Katie come in to tea, Mrs O'Brien? It's rather a
    special occasion. It's Grandfather's birthday.
Peter Sshh!
Christine No, I won't. Do you know how old he is?
John Twenty-six.

They all laugh

Christine You're just sixty years out!
Mary Ellen (*shocked*) You're not eighty-six!
Peter Yes, that's what I am, Mrs O'Brien.

Mary Ellen crosses herself

> *Katie enters with Father O'Malley*

Katie Ma, it's Father O'Malley.

There is a pause

> Ma?
Mary Ellen Good-afternoon, Father. Will you take a seat? It's dreadful
    weather. You must be wet.
John Good-afternoon, Father.
Father O'Malley Good-afternoon. (*He never takes his eyes off Peter
    Bracken*)
John Mr Bracken's a new neighbour of ours, Father.

There is a pause

Peter Father O'Malley and I already know one another.
Father O'Malley What is this man doing in your house?
Mary Ellen Well, Father——
Father O'Malley Order him to leave at once!
Mary Ellen Yes, Father . . . (*She turns to Peter*)
John Hold your hand a minute! Me da's not in, and next to him I'm head of
    this house, such as it is, and I'm telling no-one to get out, Father.
Mary Ellen John!
Father O'Malley (*looking at John*) And will you take the responsibility on
    your soul for associating with this man?
John I know nothing against the man.
Father O'Malley Then you're the only one in these parts who doesn't. This
    man is an enemy to the Catholic Church!

Peter I'm an enemy of no church!

Father O'Malley Why do you think a man of his standing is living in a quarter like this? Because he makes it his business to live among Catholics so he can turn them against the Church.

Peter I live wherever there is fear and poverty and try to erase it.

Father O'Malley Do you know what this man has dared to say? Only that he has a power equal to that of Christ! In fact, he says he is Christ!

There is a pause

Peter You know you are twisting my words! What I maintain is, we all have the power to be Christs. If we were made in God's image and likeness, then it stands to reason we are part of Him. The only difference between my spirit and God's is the size of it—the quality is exactly the same. That's what I preach. And the more I become aware of my spirit, and get in touch with it, the more God-like things I can do . . . and I have done God-like things . . . you know I have!

Father O'Malley Silence! (*To John*) Are you asking for any more proof than that?

Christine My grandfather will prove it to him. He'll show him his own power and free him from you and your like. It's not God's will that he or anyone else should live in poverty and ignorance all their days. But people mustn't think for themselves, must they? It wouldn't do for them to realize there's no purgatory or heaven or hell but what they make themselves!

Peter (*pulling her back to him*) Stay calm, Christine. Remember, anger poisons.

Father O'Malley The day is not far hence when you both shall rot in hell for your blasphemy!

Peter The day is not far hence when your sect will be fighting for its life. For there are seeds in the wombs of women at this moment that in thirty, forty or fifty years' time will shake the foundations of your preaching. People are searching for the truth—they are reading. And what do they read first? The very books that are forbidden by your Church! For the first question they ask is: why have these books been forbidden?

A long pause

Father O'Malley (*to Mary Ellen*) I leave you and your conscience to be the judge. And remember, I am warning you . . . disaster and damnation follow this man. If you wish to save your immortal soul and those of your family, throw him out as you would a snake!

He exits through the front door

Mary Ellen Yes, Father.

An awkward silence

Dominic Don't take any notice of him. He thinks he's still in Ireland.

Mick enters

Mick Ma, me ear's still runnin' and it's aching something awf——(*He stops on seeing Peter Bracken and John together*)
Peter Mrs O'Brien, I will show you! Your boy has earache, probably an abscess. I will cure it. (*He steps towards Mick*)
Mary Ellen No!

Mary Ellen tries to intercede. Mick ducks away from Peter. Mary Ellen falls and she is hurt badly. She has set the baby off and is in great internal pain

John Ma! Ma? Can you hear me?

Dominic, Mick and Katie try to get to her

Get out the way. Stand back. Give her air, for Christ's sake. It's all right, Ma. Don't move. Don't try to move. (*He picks her up*) Katie, sort the bed in the front. Mick, fetch the doctor.
Mick But, me ear . . .
John Mick!

Mick goes

Katie, go with him, will you?
Katie Me shoes? I haven't——
John They'll do. (*He throws Katie her shoe*) Just follow him, will you?

Katie goes

Dom . . . the bed.

John and Dominic lift Mary Ellen on to the bed. Dominic goes into the kitchen

Mary Ellen John, it'll be all right. I'll be all right. Don't worry . . . lad. Don't . . . John . . . (*She groans with a sharp pain and faints*)

John looks to Peter and Christine. They enter the bedroom. Peter lays his hand on Mary Ellen. Dominic looks to John, he disapproves. He goes to interfere. John stops him

Dominic goes out the back

Peter I'll go and work at her head through the wall.

Christine nods

You take her hand and don't let go. (*He places Mary Ellen's hand in Christine's, settles her*) Hold on to Christine, Mrs O'Brien. Hold tight and the pain will go. Keep holding.

He touches Christine's head and goes

The Musician starts to play on the bowed psaltery. He is highlighted in a spot. This is a surreal form of instrumentation as opposed to a melodic one

Christine is now in a form of trance and her concentration is not broken until the end of this scene. The next section is highly stylized

The following enter in the back structure and are almost silhouettes and shadows: Father O'Malley UL *on a level, Bella Bradley* UL *on a level, Peggy Flaherty* R *up a level, Nancy Kelly* UL *on a level, Musician* UR *on a level, Three women* C *of bridge level*

As the above is happening and O'Malley begins to speak, the following happens:

> *Shane enters, followed by Molly, Mick and Katie*

John turns them back from the bedroom. The kids sit in the scullery, Shane on a chair in the kitchen. The Lights then isolate: Mary Ellen and Christine in the bedroom; John and Shane in the kitchen; Molly, Katie and Mick in the scullery; Peter Bracken L *up a level, sitting in a chair, concentrating his will on Christine and Mary Ellen. The above are stronger lit than the other partici-pants in this scene but not realistically*

Father O'Malley What is this man doing in your house?
Women (*calling gently to her*) Mary Ellen. Mary . . .
Father O'Malley What is this man doing in your house?
Peggy Are you all right, Mary Ellen?
Father O'Malley I'm warning you.
Bella Who wants a bairn at forty-five I ask you?

The women laugh

> She should have been more cute . . .

The women laugh

Peggy Are you all right, Mary Ellen?
Father O'Malley If you wish to save your immortal soul and those of your family . . .
Peter That's good, Mary Ellen, good, keep holding . . .
Father O'Malley Throw him out as you would a snake!
Women Eeeh, my God!
Peter Keep holding . . . good . . . good Mary Ellen.

> *Dominic enters through the front door with a jug of beer. Hannah Kelly follows with a blanket and bowl, sees Christine*

Hannah I see . . .

Christine doesn't react

> Now look . . .

Hannah looks to him. Dominic shakes his head, gestures to the kitchen

> Oh . . . (*She tends to Mary Ellen*)

Bella Nowt good'll come of this I'm telling you.
Father O'Malley He says he has the power equal to that of Christ!
Woman 3 Spooks!
Father O'Malley In fact he says he is Christ!
Woman 2 Spooks!
Father O'Malley He says he is Christ!
Woman 1 Spooks!

Bella That lass is as bad as the old man.
Father O'Malley Christ!
Bella Lay his hands on her, that's what he said!
Father O'Malley Christ!
Bella Nowt good'll come of this ...
Women (*together, in agreement*) Spooks!
Peter Hold on, Mary.

A Doctor has entered through the back to Christine and Mary Ellen. He inspects Mary Ellen. He tries to loosen Mary Ellen's grip on Christine, but fails

Doctor You're Bracken's granddaughter, aren't you?

No response

Hannah Ay, she is, Doctor.
Doctor (*looking at Mary Ellen's eyes, looking at Christine*) Ay well there's stranger things in heaven and earth than this world dreams of, and ... I'm not going to despise your help because I'm going to need it.

He shakes his head and goes out of the front door

Kids (*on tape underneath the following*)
                    The O'Briens are fighting,
                    Do they ever stop,
                    The fight'll go on all the night,
                    Till someone gets the chop.

During the following, Shane goes into the bedroom and stands at the end of the bed

Bella It's the old windbag and Dominic!
Peggy Are you all right, Mary Ellen?
Bella It's the old windbag and Dominic!
Peggy Are you all right, Mary Ellen?
Women (*gasping*) Eeeh! My God!
Bella She's soft her, soft as clarts.
Peter Keep holding, Mary Ellen. Keep holding.
Shane (*whispering*) Oh, lass ... Mary ... Mary Ellen ... don't go ... please, lass, don't leave us ... lass ... lass. (*He pulls himself together and returns to the kitchen*)
Bella She's soft her, soft as clarts.

The kids are heard on tape. They start softly repeating "The O'Briens are fighting" underneath the following. The women say Hail Marys with rosaries, throughout the following

Father Bailey enters through the kitchen and goes to Mary Ellen. He starts praying with Hannah

Nancy Eeeh, Dominic, I haven't got a lad!
Bella Who wants a bairn at forty-five I ask you?
Nancy I haven't ... !

Bella She should have been more cute!
Nancy I don't let them come near me!
Bella She should have been more cute!
Nancy I haven't! If they comes near me I yells I do!
Peter No, Mary Ellen. Keep holding . . . Mary Ellen? Don't let go . . . don't let go.

Father Bailey finishes praying. Hannah tries to break the grip. Father Bailey stops her

Father Bailey (*looking at Christine*) Ay, well . . . God's ways are many and mysterious. He has made them, only he can judge them.

Suddenly Mary Ellen tightens her grip and Christine gives a sharp intake of breath

Father Bailey notices this, crosses himself and leaves via the kitchen, touching Shane on the shoulder as he passes. During the following, the Doctor enters through the front door

Father O'Malley If you want to save your immortal soul . . .
Woman 1 Throw him out . . . (*She crosses herself*)
Father O'Malley If you want to save your immortal soul . . .
Woman 2 Throw him out . . . (*She crosses herself*)
Father O'Malley If you want to save your immortal soul, throw him out as you would a snake!
Women Eeeh, my God!

Women 1, 2, 3 exit during the following

Kids (*on tape, singing*)
          Catholic, Catholic, ring the bell.
          When you die you'll go to hell.
Peter (*with great urgency*) Mary Ellen!

The Doctor finishes checking. He looks to Christine, then to Hannah. Hannah shakes her head. The Doctor moves to the kitchen to John's light. John pays him

Doctor Well it's touch and go really. There's not a lot I can do, losing the child has weakened her but . . . well I must warn you it doesn't look good. No, not at all, but we'll see. Tell me, do you believe in spiritual healing?
John I'm a Catholic. (*He hands the Doctor some money*)
Doctor So am I. So am I, and well . . . I'm dead against it professionally or otherwise . . . yet she seems . . . anyway we'll know by the morning.

He goes via the back door

Shane (*to John*) I don't care who keeps her alive, it can be the devil himself as long as she doesn't leave me.
John Da? (*He doesn't know what to say*) She'll pull through . . . she's strong . . . stronger than she looks.
Shane Ay . . .

Peter Now! Hold on. Mary, hold . . . yes good.

Hannah moves through to John

Hannah I'm off over home a minute, lad, and get our Joe up for work, then I'll be back.

John (*nodding*) Any change?

Hannah I don't know . . . perhaps a little . . . she's breathing easier. Pity she lost the bairn though.

John Is it?

Hannah John! . . . That's a terrible . . . Ay, well maybe you're right. Funny thing about the lass, though. Your ma hanging on to her like that. After she said she'd have nowt to do with them. She's had me scared stiff sitting so still. 'Tisn't natural, is it? It's a rum do.

He nods

What are you going to do if it goes on any longer?

John I don't know.

Hannah Ay well there's queerer things happen, I suppose, but if so, I don't know what.

Hannah goes

Father O'Malley I leave you and your conscience to be the judge!

Nancy Goodbye, Mrs O'Brien!

Bella Soft as clarts!

Peggy And remember if you want any advice, Mary Ellen, you know where to come.

Nancy, Bella, Peggy and O'Malley exit

The music soars. Mary Ellen releases Christine's hand. Peter and Christine relax the tension in their bodies. Both are exhausted. John enters the bedroom. He sees the grip is broken and looks to Christine

Christine She's asleep . . . the worst is over. She's past the crisis, all she needs now is rest.

Peter with some effort rises and goes

John Come into the kitchen.

Christine I can't yet. I've got cramp. I'm stiff. In a little while.

Hannah enters from the front

Hannah She's let go then. (*She checks Mary Ellen*) You'd better get yourself away to bed, lass.

Christine tries to rise, helped by John

John You're all in. Come on, let me take you home.

Christine's legs give way on her a little, John saves her from falling

Christine It's the cramp . . . it'll be a while before my legs belong to me

again. Only temporary, I'll be all right in the morning. I'm tired that's all.
John There's only one thing for it then. (*He picks her up in his arms, makes to go out the front*) I think we'd better go through the yard.
Christine Yes.

He takes her into the kitchen, stops

You're a good man, John ... (*She is falling asleep*)
John (*smiling at her*) Ay, well don't let it get about.

They go

Hannah (*referring to John and Christine*) Ay, well you can never tell where blisters'll light. But, my God, won't Mary Ellen go mad!

The music soars. The Lights change. The O'Brien truck rolls back

SCENE 10

As the O'Brien house rolls back, the music crossfades to church organ music. A church window flies in

We see Katie standing in a sharp pool of light R. She is crying and frightened. John is isolated in a pool of light L, looking off R. He is waiting for Katie

Father Bailey enters C. He has a little stool and sits C, isolated in a pool of light

The light fades on John. Father Bailey rings a small handbell and Katie enters to him. They are in the confessional

The music fades into the background

Katie Please, Father, give me thy blessing for I have sinned. It is three weeks since my last confession.
Father Bailey Go on, my child.
Katie I have missed Mass once.
Father Bailey Through your own fault?
Katie No, Father. It was me clothes. Me ma wouldn't let me come.
Father Bailey Go on, my child.
Katie I have spoken in church and I have missed me morning and night prayers.
Father Bailey How often?
Katie Three times ... no, four ... perhaps a few more, Father.
Father Bailey Why?
Katie 'Cos the lino's cracked and it sticks in me knees when I kneel down.
Father Bailey (*clearing his throat and biting his lip, amused*) It is important that you say your prayers—prayers are the food of the soul, like bread is the food of the body ... you understand, my child?
Katie Yes, Father.
Father Bailey Then under no circumstances should you starve your soul.
Katie No, Father.

Father Bailey Go on.

Silence

Is there anything more?
Katie Yes, Father.
Father Bailey Well, then, what is it?

Silence

Don't be afraid, my child. There is nothing so terrible that God won't forgive.
Katie I stole.
Father Bailey You what? (*He is shocked. He knows Katie. He tries to look at her through the grille*)
Katie I stole.
Father Bailey What did you steal?
Katie A "Rainbow".
Father Bailey A what?
Katie A comic.
Father Bailey (*amused, biting his tongue again*) Now, my child, you know how it hurts our Blessed Lord when you do anything like that.
Katie Yes, Father.
Father Bailey And will you do it again?
Katie No, no. Never, Father.
Father Bailey No, I know you won't. And if you could find a way to pay the shopkeeper for the comic, it would put everything right, wouldn't it?
Katie Yes, Father.
Father Bailey Now for your penance, say one Our Father and ten Hail Marys, and tell our Lord that never again will you hurt him, and he will forgive you. And don't forget to kneel when you are saying your prayers, in spite of the lino, for remember the nails on the cross. (*He makes the sign of the cross and mutters the absolution*)
Katie Oh, my God, I am very sorry I have sinned against Thee because Thou art so good and by the help of Thy Holy Grace I will never sin again.
Father Bailey Good-night, my child, and God bless you. And worry no more. He understands.

Katie stands, smiles, runs off R

Father Bailey tinkles the little handbell. No-one comes, so he goes. As Father Bailey is going . . .

A Light comes up on John. He is waiting for Katie

Katie runs to him as if she hasn't seen him in years

Katie Oh, John! John.

He swings her round

Are you going to go to Confession now?

John No. But if it works miracles like this, I might consider it again. Has Father Bailey given you a pair of wings?

Katie No, but he's so nice. I won't be crying anymore, John.

John Well, thank the Lord for that. What was wrong with you, anyway?

Katie I stole.

John (*stunned*) You what?

Katie I stole.

John You?

Katie Yes ... I stole a comic from Mr Powell's.

John You? You stole ...

Katie Yes. But now I've confessed and Father Bailey says it's all right.

John You stole a comic?

Katie nods

Have you done it before?

Katie No, only that once ...

John Katie?

Katie Honest, John, I haven't.

John Why did you do it?

Katie I hadn't had a comic for weeks, and I hadn't a ha'penny, so I——

John (*grabbing her*) Don't you ever do that again, ever! Do you hear me?

She shakes her head

Ever! Promise me, you'll never do that again.

She nods

If you want a comic, ask me. Understand? Come to me.

She nods. Pause. He throws her aside roughly and tries to calm himself down

Katie (*tugging his sleeve*) I'm sorry, John ... really, I am ... John?

John Tell me about this exam.

Katie What?

John This exam your teacher's on about. What do you have to do?

Katie I told you. You said it was nothing to do with you.

John Well, tell me now. I want to know.

John goes. Katie follows

Katie (*puzzled*) Well, Miss Llewellyn says that if I ...

The Lights change

SCENE 11

Light classical piano music plays on tape

Three maids and a footman enter and set Mary Llewellyn's drawing-room—a sofa, an armchair, somewhere a model of a yacht and a statue of a naked lady. A large draped window is flown in behind. The servants exit

John is led in by a Maid. He has on a new overcoat and is well out of his depth

Maid You'd better wait in here. This is Miss Mary's room. It is Miss Mary you've come to see?
John Ay, the teacher.
Maid Is she expecting you?
John No.
Maid What did you say your name was?
John O'Brien.
Maid O'Br—— (*She's heard of the O'Briens*) I'll tell her you're here.

She goes

John nervously fingers his clothes, looks round the room. He is impressed. He goes to sit, nervous, he decides to sit in the chair. The music stops

Mary enters

He stands quickly

Mary Hello, Mr O'Brien.
John Hello ...

They shake hands

Mary Is everything all right?
John Oh, ay ... yes, fair enough.
Mary Good. I'm glad to hear it. Well, you wanted to see me?
John Ay ... yes.
Mary I presume then you've come to talk about Katie?
John Ay ... yes.
Mary Good. Come and sit down. I'm so glad you've come for I'd like to know what plans you have for her.

They sit

Now, would you like her to become a teacher?
John Yes.
Mary Well, I'm glad of that.
John Yes ... if it's possible ... that is.
Mary Oh, I think so. She's a bright girl.
John Yes.
Mary And even if she only becomes an uncertified teacher, it would be something, wouldn't it?
John (*nodding*) Yes. Yes ...

There is a pause. John is staring at Mary

Mary (*embarrassed*) I'll speak to the Head about it.
John Yes.
Mary Em ... it is what you want for Katie, isn't it?
John Ay. Definitely ... yes. There's nothing I want more in the world for her ... I mean, if it was up to me ... I'm sorry, I'm making a mess of this ... there's so much I want to say ... and ...

Mary Take your time, there's no hurry. I've got all evening.

John Thank you ... thanks ... well, you can guess how we're fix——situated. I'll be straight with you ... there won't be any money to help her as far as I can see. If it was up to me, and I could ... but I'm rarely on full time as it is. To be honest, some weeks we only just get by with enough to eat.

Mary I understand.

John What with me da hardly fit for work now. And there's Molly and Mick as well as Katie ... and, well, Molly will be working in another year but it'll be a while before we can get Mick on the docks ... So, you see ... well, I suppose I'm telling you all this to put you in the picture, like. To make it plain that if Katie becoming a teacher depends on money, even in the future, well, we haven't any. And I don't really see how in that case it's possible. And I'd rather for her sake we started to get her used to the idea now. Not to get her hopes up, like. So ... well, that's it, really.

Mary Thank you.

John Well, I ...

Mary Thank you for being so honest.

John Well, it's no good pretending, is it? (*He starts to go*)

Mary No. But I'm sure that together we'll find a way round it. Would you like to take your coat off and we can make ourselves comfortable and talk the whole thing out. Would you like some tea?

John Er, yes, thanks.

She goes

He takes his coat off, carefully places it on a chair, looks at his suit

Well, she was never really going to be fooled by a pawnshop coat, John, lad. Tea with Miss Llewellyn, eh?

She enters

Mary It'll be along in a minute. (*She sits*) Now, where were we? Oh, yes, money. Right. Well, that question won't really arise until Katie is a little older.

The Lights fade to a half-light on John and Mary

The Musician is highlighted in the back structure, playing

The Maid enters with a tray set for tea. She pours, hands a cup to Mary

John awkwardly takes his tea from the Maid

The Maid goes

Mary stands, walks to the back. The Lights come up again. Mary and John are laughing. About an hour has passed

(*Quoting*) "A day of high winds and far mastheads and bonnie lasses." (*She laughs*) Now, when I find phrases like that in Katie's composition ... or this, "The morning sky was massed with white clouds like brakes ready for a day off." Though I know she's clever, she's not that clever. They are yours, aren't they?

John (*with an embarrassed laugh*) Yes.

Mary (*laughing*) I was as sorry as she when I had to make her scrap the composition in which she stated that "ore on her tongue and sweat in her hair and bleeding nails meant gold on a Saturday and roaming round the market, hemmed in with the smells of tallow and the flapping of skirts."

John I'll have to be more careful what I say ... you see we go for walks.

Mary I know, I saw you, remember? You looked like you'd just seen a ghost.

John You weren't quite what I'd imagined.

Mary I wasn't quite the dragon you'd expected?

John (*laughing*) Compared with my old teacher, you're more like a fairy princess.

Mary (*laughing*) Thank you. Tell that to some of my pupils. I meant what I said, though, you should try writing them down.

John (*embarrassed*) No ...

Mary A lot of men write poetry, you know.

He laughs

It's a talent.

John (*deeply embarrassed*) I can't even speak properly.

Mary Oh, please don't say that.

John It's true.

Mary You don't speak any differently from anybody else. And besides that has nothing to do with putting your thoughts on paper.

John (*sarcastically*) I've been told there's such a thing as grammar.

Mary Yes, but that comes ... you learn as you go.

John Ay, well. Thank you for your patience and help about Katie. It's a relief, I can tell you ... I'd best be off now ... Saturday isn't the most convenient time to call.

Mary No, no, please. You haven't finished your tea yet, and I'm not going out this evening. And anyway I want to know more about Mr Bracken and Christine. Is he really eighty-six?

John Ay. Ma thinks it's something to do with the devil, looking so good at that age.

Mary I get them every day on the way to school. (*Mimicking Katie*) "Oh, Christine's wonderful! And Christine has a wonderful house, and cooks wonderful food, and has wonderful clothes ... Ooh, she's wonderful."

John (*can't help laughing*) I'm afraid Katie thinks a number of people are wonderful. (*He looks at her*) Not that she isn't right most of the time.

They smile at each other. A short silence develops

Well ... I ... (*He makes to go*)

Mary Are you interested in boats? I mean the building of them?

John I know nothing about building them. Only that I get certain feelings working in them. Friendliness for some ... dislike for others. I suppose it has a lot to do with their cargo ... (*He laughs*) "The sweat in my hair."

Mary Come and look at this one. My father hopes to build her someday.
She's quite unlike all the others in his workshop . . . what is it?
John (*stunned*) Your father's Llewellyn the boat-builder, then?
Mary Yes. Didn't you know?
John No. I didn't put the two together, that's all.
Mary (*looking at the boat*) She's beautiful, isn't she?
John (*still looking at Mary*) Yes . . . yes . . . she is.

She looks at him and smiles

Well, I'd best be off.
Mary But I was going to show you round the workshop . . .
John No, thanks. I'd better go. Thanks again for your time and patience . . .
you must be quite busy and I don't want to intrude and—— (*He almost
trips over the octaroon*) Oh, sorry . . . (*He stares at the statue*)
Mary I came across her in an antique shop in Newcastle. Mother wouldn't
have it in the house, but as she never comes in here permission was finally
granted. The servants look the other way when dusting. Does it shock
you?
John I think it's very beautiful.
Mary Thank you. So do I.

There is a pause

The Maid enters

Maid Miss?
Mary Yes, Phyliss?
Maid Mr Culbert is downstairs.
Mary Gilbert? Ask him to wait, will you.

The Maid goes

He's a friend of the family. He often drops in unexpectedly. Mother is
very fond of him, you see.
John Well, thanks . . .
Mary For the third time? Or is it four?
John Sorry. But it has been kind of you to spare the time. I'll be off.
Mary I'll see you out.

The Lights change. They are in a pool of light downstage. Music starts

Servants strike the Llewellyn set during the following

Well, good-night, Mr O'Brien. If there is ever a time when you want to
talk about Katie, or anything else for that matter, do call round. I'm very
fond of Katie, you know. She's a clever child.
John She's got a good teacher.
Mary Thank you.
Maid (*off; calling*) Miss . . .
Mary (*sharply*) I'm coming! . . . Good-night.

She goes

John (*alone in light*) Well, Katie O'Brien, that's you set! And another thing you're right on. Miss Llewellyn is "wonderful". (*He laughs*)

The Lights change. The music goes

Nancy Kelly enters on the opposite side of the stage, crying

(*Crossing to her*) Hello, Nancy. What's the matter?

Nancy (*scared at first, then recognizing him*) Eeeh, John. Eeeh, John.

John What's the matter?

Nancy It's our Annie. She left me in the market—she run away and she had me tram fare. An' me ma'll skelp me when I get in. She will, 'cos Mrs Fitzsimmons said I had to be back to clean out the shop when they closed. An' me ma said our Annie had to put me on the tram that takes me to me place.

John Now, stop crying. You'll be back in plenty of time. There's your tram fare—and a penny to buy some bullets. Stand over there. The Jarrow tram will be along in a minute.

Nancy Eeeh, I can't get the tram there, John. There's a bar there an' me mam says I've got to keep away from bars 'cos the men come out.

John (*putting out his hand for her to hold*) Come on, then, I'll put you on it. (*As they go*) Now stop crying. Mrs Fitzsimmons is all right and she'll understand even if you are late . . .

They exit

SCENE 12

The kids enter singing "We Wish You a Merry Christmas". They sing the first verse up to Bella's level. No response. They shout out the verse again

Bella enters on level L

Bella (*throwing two coins*) There's a penny, now, stop your screeching and go and pester someone else for a change!

The kids dive for the coins

And you needn't bother passing the word to your friends. Christmas Eve or not that's all you'll get from me!

The kids exit R *singing*

Bella exits

The O'Brien truck rolls forward. The Lights change. Peggy is sitting in the kitchen. Mary Ellen is baking mince pies

Peggy Well, is he or isn't he?

Mary Ellen Courting, our John?

Peggy Ay, it happens, you know! Has he said owt?

Mary Ellen No. Mind you, he's been full of himself this past month or two.

Peggy Well, there you are, then. Now, I don't want to speak his turn, but I've seen him at least three times over this last month, and the last no later than this dinner-time, talking to the same lass.

Mary Ellen Who?

Peggy Well, she's not from round these doors. She had a fur coat on her the day and the number of tails hanging from the collar alone must have left a number of poor animals feeling cold around their backsides.

Mary Ellen A fur coat?

Peggy Ay, and a voice like the gentry, for I heard her as I passed.

Mary Ellen It can't have been him.

Peggy I'm telling ye. He called out to me himself.

Mary Ellen (*referring to next door*) It wasn't ... ?

Peggy I may be short of sight, Mary Ellen, but I'm not blind. This was a bonny big lump of a lass. In fact, she's a woman, and twice the size of that stick next door.

Hannah enters through the front door

Hannah Bloody weather! The only ones enjoying it are the bairns. Oh, hello, Peggy.

Mary Ellen Sit down, lass. I'll make some tea.

Hannah Not now, thanks all the same. I only came over to see you a minute ... about something. (*She refers to Peggy*)

Peggy I'll off up, Mary Ellen. I must make a start. I'm up to me eyes upstairs.

She goes

Hannah Eeeh. How she lives among all that junk, God alone knows.

Mary Ellen Is anything wrong, Hannah?

Hannah It's our Nancy. I've had a letter from Mrs Fitzsimmons about her. She says she won't do the work. She's gone all stubborn on her. That isn't like Nancy, you know. I mean, as bad as she is, she can do the rough work of half a dozen and likes it. She says she'll have to send her home if it carries on ... Oh, Mary Ellen, it'll be murder with our Joe if she's in the house all the time.

Mary Ellen Ay, well maybe you can get her in some place else.

Hannah Not if she won't work, I won't. She's hard work at the best of times. You and John are the only ones who treat her like a human being. I know I don't. Sometimes I can't stand the sight of her. I know that's a terrible thing to say, but it's true. I try and protect her from our Joe, but——

Dominic enters in a fury. He throws his gear down in the kitchen, and goes into the front to change

Dominic I want my tea now. I'm going out! (*He goes to the front room*)

Hannah Who's been biting him today?

Mary Ellen Look, Hannah, I'll pop over later and maybe we can have a cup of tea.

Hannah Thanks, Mary Ellen. I hope you don't mind me coming across and telling ye, but you're the only one I seem to be able to talk to about her.
Mary Ellen I'll see you later, lass.

Hannah goes

What's up with you, then?
Dominic I want me tea now. (*He is in the front room*)
Mary Ellen Can't you get changed first and have it with the others?
Dominic (*entering the scullery and washing himself*) No, I can't! And anyway you wouldn't expect God Almighty to sit down with me, would you?
Mary Ellen What?

Dominic goes to the front room again

Here! What's up with you? The tea's not ready yet. I've some mince pies and some bread and dripping if you're in a hurry. (*She puts them on the table*)
Dominic (*entering and looking at the plate*) That's a fine meal for a man, isn't it?
Mary Ellen Well, you wouldn't wait. I'm going to fry.
Dominic (*snatching a piece of bread from her*) You're going to fry! Well, see that you do plenty of it. The big pot'll need it to fill his swelled head.

He storms out of the front door

She listens. There is a knock next door

Molly and Katie enter

Molly Ma! Ma! Ma, our Katie's dirtied her knickers.
Mary Ellen What!

Molly and Katie burst out laughing

Molly Eeh, no! Not that way. She slipped on a slide and ended up in some broken ice and slush.
Mary Ellen Are you wet?
Katie No, Ma, it dried.
Mary Ellen Tea won't be for some time yet. Here, take a bit of bread and get yourselves out again.

They grab the bread and go

(*Calling*) You can stay out another half-hour or so. And hunt up our Mick and bring him back with you. (*She busies herself*)

John enters

John Anybody in?
Mary Ellen Oh, John! What is it, what's happened?
John I'll give you three guesses.
Mary Ellen Eeh, no, John, stop messing about . . .

John Go on ...
Mary Ellen John ...
John Mrs O'Brien, behold a gaffer!
Mary Ellen (*shocked*) Eeeh, no ...
John (*grinning*) Ay, takes a bit of getting used to, doesn't it?
Mary Ellen The men picked you?
John Ay, to take old Reville's place.
Mary Eeeh, John ...
John Ay.
Mary Ellen A gaffer ...! Were all the men with you?
John Not all, but the ones that mattered were.
Mary Was none of the others after it?
John Ay. But none of them were steady.
Mary Ellen And they voted for you?
John Ay.
Mary Ellen Eeeh, John ... a gaffer ... does your da know?
John He took it all right.
Mary Ellen Eeeh, a gaffer ... John ... (*She is crying*)
John (*taking her in his arms*) Hey, come here ...

There is a loud banging of a door, off. Mary Ellen starts

Dominic?
Mary Ellen Ay. He went next door again.

John sighs

Molly enters

Molly Ma! Ma, our Katie's wet her knickers again!

Katie enters, holding the back of her dress away from her behind

John and Mary Ellen burst out laughing

SCENE 13

The Lights change and a tape of a brass band and a crowd of people singing "O Come All Ye Faithful" is heard

The cast enter accompanying the tape and set up market stalls

The left and right parts of the main O'Brien house truck split off and roll back leaving the kitchen. Mary Ellen rearranges the kitchen whilst this is happening, then starts knitting. She remains visible in the centre of the market throughout the next scene, which takes place around her. All the cast play stallholders and shoppers. The lighting should be somewhat stylized to maintain these two realities. John, who entered with the crowd, is standing somewhere counting his money. As the market settles, one man is still singing out loud, obviously drunk

His wife enters

Woman Found you! You bugger. I knew it! I bloody knew it!
Man Merry Christmas!
Woman (*hitting him and pushing him off*) Not bloody yet it isn't.
Man Give us a kiss!
Woman (*hitting him*) And that's all the kiss you'll be getting till next Christmas.
Man Why you ...
Woman (*hitting him again*) Home now. (*Pushing him out*) I've been in every tap house in Shields looking for you! (*She hits him*) Where's the bloody shopping, eh? Where's the money? So help me if you've drunk your bonus ...

They exit and there is a loud slap, off

Man (*off*) Ooow!
Woman (*off*) And there's a lot more where that come from!

The rest of the market laugh. One of the kids shouts out "Merry Christmas!" A woman stallholder boxes his ears

Mary enters and sees John

The Lights change to isolate the following scene DC. The market people continue action but minimize any extraneous noise

Mary John! Well, what a pleasant surprise! Hello, again, twice in one day. It must be an omen.
John Hello ...
Mary Doing your last-minute shopping?
John No ... yes ... well ... I'm ... (*He grins*) I'm hanging around until they give the ducks away on the market.
Mary Do they do that?
John Yes, if you catch them at the last minute. They're desperate to be rid of them, cheap, like. Especially on Christmas Eve.
Mary (*laughing*) Yes, I'd like to see this lot trying to eat their way through all those turkeys tomorrow.
John (*laughing*) Some of them look as if they already have.

They laugh

Mary You know, we'll have to stop meeting like this or people will talk.
John Don't think they aren't already.
Mary What? Oh, dear, Peggy Flaherty?
John I did warn you. By this time they'll have us wed and a family to boot.

She laughs

Ma was giving me a queer look the night an' all.
Mary Does it bother you?
John It was you I was thinking of. "The school teacher and the docker." Bella Bradley'd think it was her birthday!
Mary (*laughing*) Occupational hazard, I'm afraid. The intrigues which are accredited to yours truly through the imagination of the parents and children you just wouldn't believe, Mr O'Brien.

John Oh, I can imagine.

Mary Well, I'd best be off, John. Merry——

John Look ...

Mary Yes?

John Well ... can I carry your parcels to the tram for you?

Mary Well, I wasn't going home yet.

John Oh, I see. All right, then.

Mary But if you're not busy it would be a relief if you'd help me with them.

John Certainly. The ducks are well out of my range at the moment.

Mary (*giving him parcels*) My arms are dropping off, and I've only a little more shopping to do. I don't think I'll ask you to carry this one.

John Oh, no bother.

She shakes her head. John looks at the package

What is it?

Mary (*whispering*) Lingerie.

John What? Oh, ay, right. Fair enough.

Mary I thought as much. (*She laughs*) Well, Mr O'Brien, all you need now is a white beard and a red cloak and you've a job for the night.

John Eh? Oh, ay. (*He grins at her*)

There is a pause

Mary (*turning*) Well, then, follow me, Santa.

John Look ...

Mary Yes?

John (*clearing his throat*) How about ... would you care to go to a variety show or the pantomime?

Mary I'd love to, Mr O'Brien.

John Pardon?

Mary I'd love to.

John (*grinning*) Fine! Right! I thought we could get some bullets ... I mean, chocolates. (*He nearly drops the parcels*) A box of chocolates, and we'll make a night of it.

Mary Wonderful. Where shall we go?

John Wherever you like.

Mary Anywhere.

John I'm easy. Empire or Tivoli?

Mary Whichever you want.

John I'm not bothered. I'm paying, you decide.

Mary All right. Done. Oh, is there time for me to make a telephone call?

John A telephone call?

Mary I'll have to ring Father.

John Where do you go for that? The post office?

Mary Yes. I won't be more than five minutes, I promise.

John Right then, come on. Oh, what about the rest of your shopping?

Mary (*taking his arm*) Oh, I think the shopping can wait, don't you? We'll do it later. Come on.

They go

The Lights change. There is the sound of a brass band and the cast singing "The Holly and the Ivy" on tape

The cast clear the market and exit

Scene 14

Mary Ellen is in the kitchen, asleep

John enters. He is whistling carols, loaded down with parcels. It is late. He is in a rush to get out and full of himself

Mary Ellen John!

John (*whispering*) Merry Christmas, Ma! (*He puts the large box on the table*)

Mary Ellen In the name of God, have you bought the market?

John You'll never guess what that is ... it's a turkey!

Mary Ellen A turkey!

John Ay, ay. And this is a bag of fruit. And there's bullets in that box, and ... (*he hands her a sprig of holly*) ... Merry Christmas, Ma.

Mary Ellen Oh, John, you've never had a drink?

John Drink? (*He laughs loud*) You know me better than that. Stop looking so worried, Ma. We ... I waited till the very last minute and I got him for four bob. Daylight robbery, eh, Ma? Merry Christmas!

Mary Ellen A stone bag of fruit! Are they specked?

John I should say not. She ... (*He starts combing his hair*) Miss Llewellyn sent them for the bairns.

Mary Ellen Miss Llewellyn?

John Ay, I bumped into her in the market.

Mary Ellen Did you, now?

John I can't stop, Ma. I'm going up to Midnight Mass in Jarrow.

Mary Ellen Midnight ... ? You're going to church?

John Ay. Nothing wrong with that, is there?

Mary Ellen No ... no.

John I'll have to get a move on ...

Mary Ellen John?

John The last tram'll be at the end of the street in a minute.

Mary Ellen John?

John What? I've got to go, Ma.

Mary Ellen Be careful.

John Oh, Ma. (*He laughs*) Worried about me, are you?

Mary Ellen Just be careful! (*She busies herself*)

John Ma ... (*He looks at her*)

Mary Ellen Well, go on, you'd better go if you're going.

John (*grinning at her*) Ay. (*He kisses her*) Merry Christmas, Ma!

John goes

The Lights isolate Mary Ellen during the following. She is touched by the kiss, but very worried

Mary Ellen Eeeh, our John . . . a gaffer isn't a boat-builder. Miss "beautiful" Llewellyn, that's all we need. You hurt my boy with your games and
I'll have more than a few words to say to you, lass, teacher or not. Eeeh,
John, you'd have more chance with that stick next door. Christmas or no,
there's a limit. (*She laughs*) Midnight Mass! Eeeh, our John, I'd laugh, but
it's not funny. Please, Lord, don't hurt the lad . . . don't let her hurt him.
Midnight Mass! My God. (*She laughs*)

The Lights change

The Musician plays something haunting on the flute

Mary Ellen is isolated, busy unpacking John's shopping

*John and Mary cross through the back structure. They are walking
separately. They occasionally stop as John points out something to her in
the distance. They exit*

The Lights change, isolating the Musician. He finishes

CURTAIN

ACT II

As the house lights go down, a tape of people singing "Auld Lang Syne" is heard—not a choir, just a group of people celebrating

Underneath this, the CURTAIN *rises to reveal the Llewellyn household. Servants are in evidence—three maids, a butler and a footman. It is after dinner on New Year's Eve and there is a lot of unspoken tension in the household*

Eventually the servants are dismissed

The music fades. In the drawing-room are Beatrice, James and Mary

Beatrice Well, and what have you to say for yourself, madam?

James Look, Beatrice, leave this to me.

Beatrice Too much has been left to you and look at the result! As for you, I don't know how you have the effrontery to stand there and look me in the eye! No wonder you wouldn't tell me who you were with on Christmas Eve! It is to your credit that you were ashamed.

Mary I'm not.

Beatrice What's that?

Mary I'm not ashamed. I just knew how you'd react, that's all.

Beatrice You must have lost every spark of decency. You never, at any time, had a proper sense of what is correct. But this! Have you any idea how I felt when Florence Dudley told me they saw you in the Empire with a . . . docker? Will Dudley says he comes from the fifteen streets and the family are notorious.

Mary Of course they are. Anyone within a three miles radius of the fifteen streets knows that. If you didn't shut out every unpleasantness from your life, you would have heard it before . . .

Beatrice Mary, I can't believe that even with your liberal tastes you could sink so low as to associate with a notorious——

Mary One of the main things for which they are notorious is hunger. Dwell on that the next time you're preparing for the Dudleys coming to dinner.

Beatrice They are poor because they drink and gamble. And you! You are a slut! You were out with that man until three o'clock in the morning. Do you think it won't be all around Jarrow and Shields by now?

Mary I hope so.

James Here, lass, that's enough!

Beatrice (*enraged*) You low creature! You're utterly debased. I shall have Father O'Malley to you. Yes. Yes, I shall . . .

James tries to soothe her

Leave me alone!

She storms out of the room

There is a pause

James You've done it this time. You know, lass, it was a bit of a shock.
Mary (*sharply*) To you too?
James Ay ... yes. It's no good saying one thing and thinking another. But when Will Dudley got on about seeing you with one of the big O'Briens, I could have punched him in the face. I could tell it had afforded them a good topic of conversation all the week, and that was why Florence Dudley was so anxious for us to drop in this morning. When your mother came downstairs with her, I thought she'd collapse ... How long has this been going on, lass?
Mary It hasn't been "going on", as you call it. That was the only time.
James (*relieved*) Oh ... well ... and are you ... well, is it finished?
Mary I don't know.
James You don't know! What do you mean, lass?
Mary I mean if it rests with me, it won't be finished. I haven't seen him since because he never asked me.
James (*after a pause*) I see ... Now, see here, you know which side I've always been on, don't you? You know that life would have been much easier for me if I'd taken your mother's part all along. But I want you to understand, lass, that I'm with your mother in this.
Mary You'd rather see me married to Gilbert, then?
James I don't want you to marry anyone you don't fancy ... but yes, yes, I'd rather see you married to Gilbert than carrying on with this business ...
Mary Well I wouldn't.
James At least you wouldn't starve. Mary ... stop while there's still time. You don't know what you're running yourself into. Lass, I hate to say it, but I've seen those O'Briens rolling from one side of the arches to the other. I even remember the mother, years ago, standing outside the bars with the bairns clinging round her, trying to get a few shillings out of her man before he blew the lot. I tell you, lass, they're noted.
Mary He doesn't drink.
James That's what he says.
Mary He doesn't, Father. And he's not just a docker, either. He's been made a gaffer.
James Did he tell you that? How old is he?
Mary (*defiantly*) Twenty-two.
James He's a damned liar! There's no fellow could be made a gaffer at twenty-two. Thirty-two would be more like it. He's kidding you, lass. Can't you see?
Mary No, he's not. Anyway, it should be easy for you to find out.
James Yes. Quite easy. But even so, if he's a gaffer, what's that?

Mary can't answer

Hinny . . . I only want your happiness. What do you think I've worked for all these years? To leave you comfortable. Look, my dear, promise me you'll drop this.

Mary (*after a pause*) I can't. If he asks me out again, I'll go.

James quietly leaves the room

Mary is upset

(*Quietly*) And a happy New Year to you too, Father.

She puts on her coat and goes

SCENE 2

Music. The Lights change

The Musician appears in the back structure playing "Blaydon Races" on the hurdy-gurdy as . . .

The servants appear and strike Llewellyn furniture. As the furniture is struck a tape joins in of a crowd of people round a bonfire singing "Blaydon Races"

At the same time, a team of young lads appears and drapes two snowcloths L and R to create one corner of a large field where off L there are hundreds of people skating. A bonfire is casting shadows from L on to the set. This is sometimes broken with shadows and movement indicating a large number of people round the various fires singing. Throughout the whole of the next scene this effect of people having a singsong continues, with snatches of "Waters of Tyne", "Bobby Shaftoe", "The Lambton Worm", "Cushy Butterfield" etc., all used to enhance the action and atmosphere. When the lads have set the snowcloths they run off L cheering and shouting, "Come on let's skate!!" etc.

John enters from R. He is dressed up to the nines and is looking around, fairly preoccupied

Katie (*off L*) John, look, look at me. Look at Christine. She's dead good, isn't she?

John (*shouting to her off*) Ay, she is! (*He claps, shouts to Christine*) Keep spinning like that you'll go through the ice!

Christine (*off L, shouting back*) Isn't it wonderful! Come on the ice, John!

John (*shouting back*) No chance!

Christine (*off*) Come on, John, I'll pull you.

John Not on your life.

Christine enters and goes to John, having come off the ice

Christine A big thing like you afraid of the ice!

John You'd be more afraid if I got on there and fell on you.

Christine (*taking his hand*) I'll risk it. Come on. Oh, John, don't be a spoilsport, please.

John No way. Sorry.

Christine Are you all right, John?

John Yes. Yes, I'm fine.

Christine John, you can't lie to me. I know there's something. You haven't
    been round to talk to Grandfather, or me for that matter, since before
    Christmas. If I didn't know better, I'd say you were avoiding us.

John I'm sorry. I just had a lot to think about. I needed to get it straight for
    myself.

Christine And is it? You don't look as if you've slept in a week.

John Yes, I think so.

Christine Do you want to talk about it?

John No.

Christine Grandfather thinks a lot of you, you know.

John Ay.

Christine He misses your talks. We'd both like you to consider us your
    friends.

John I do. I'm sorry. I had to sort this out for myself, that's all.

Christine Come and skate, then. You big silent gaffer!

She grabs him. He breaks her hold

John I've plenty of ways of making a fool of myself besides that, thank you.

Katie (*off*) John!

Katie enters from L

Christine Oh, well, suit yourself. (*She goes back towards the ice, passing
    Katie as she leaves*) Come on, Katie. Your brother is standing on his
    dignity the night!

Christine exits

Katie His what? Have you and Christine fell out, or what?

John Or what, I think.

Katie Eh? (*Whispering*) Our Dominic's along there, John. He's watching
    Christine.

John (*looking*) Has he had a drink?

Katie No, he looks all right, but he's got a collar and tie on an' all. He's got
    a new coat on, an' all, John.

John Don't forget what I told you. Don't leave them alone together.

Katie No, John, I wouldn't. Whenever I see him going next door I go round
    the back like you said and ask to borrow a book or something.

John No matter what he says on the way home, don't leave her, mind.

Katie John, why can't I leave her alone with Dominic?

John Just don't, that's all.

Katie Why?

John You haven't told her I asked you to do this?

Katie Eeeh! No, I haven't, honest, John. I think she suspects, but she's still
    pleased to see me. Our Dominic doesn't like it, though.

John Good.

Katie She likes you more than Dominic, you know.

John Go on, on your slide. I'll be around for a while yet.
Katie (*shouting, teasing as she goes*) She does, you know.

Katie goes

John Go and slide! (*He looks around at the crowd etc. He is searching for someone*)

The singing swells—"Waters of Tyne"

Mary Llewellyn enters R

John doesn't see her at first. She walks slowly to him. The singing fades. He sees her

I wondered if you'd be here.

She smiles

Have you been sliding?
Mary I haven't any skates.
John What about using your feet? It seems popular.
Mary Here?
John No. Let's go round the other side. There are fewer people there and if we fall there'll be less to laugh at us.

She agrees and they start to move

Katie enters

Katie Miss Llewellyn! Miss Llewellyn, it is you. I thought so. Hello. Happy New Year, Miss.

Christine enters behind Katie and stands a little way from them, watching

Mary Why! Hello, Katie. And a happy New Year to you too. Are you having a lovely time?
Katie Yes, Miss Llewellyn.
Mary And did you have a nice Christmas?
Katie Oh, yes, Miss Llewellyn. Lovely! And thank you for the presents and all the lovely fruit.

Mary looks to Christine

Oh, Christine, look, it's Miss Llewellyn.
John This is Christine . . .

Christine turns and goes

Katie Christine? (*To John*) Have you had a row or something?

John shakes his head

Honestly, Miss, I hope you can cheer him up. He's had a face on him like a wet weekend since Christmas. 'Bye Miss! (*As she goes*) Christine! Christine, wait for me.

She goes

There is a pause. Mary looks at John

John Christine's a nice girl ...

Mary Yes, she looks it.

John I don't think she'll ever grow up, though. She's ... well, she's just like Katie.

Mary (*smiling*) I see ...

John What about the slide? Shall we chance it?

Mary If you like.

John Do you want to slide?

Mary No.

John Would you ... would you like to go for a walk? Or what about Shields?

Mary Not Shields. Let's go for a walk.

They go off R

The singing swells—"Bobby Shaftoe"

Christine enters L. She sees Mary and John go

Dominic enters close behind her

The singing fades

Dominic Christine, come on, I only want to slide.

Christine moves downstage with him close behind

Christine For goodness' sake, Dominic. Leave me be. I'm going home. Where's Katie?

Dominic I sent her to look for Mick. What the hell's the matter with you, anyway? Don't you know how to enjoy yourself? Come on. (*He grabs her*)

Christine Dominic ... no.

Dominic No, not tonight. Tonight you're with me. Kiss me. Go on. It's not asking a lot. Come on, you know you want to. We've played this game too often.

She tries to push him away

Relax, no-one's watching us.

She kicks him and breaks free

Ow! You ...! What the hell did you do that for? You could've broken my leg.

Christine Serve you right. Now, leave me alone, please!

Dominic I don't understand you. Look, I've asked you to marry me, what else ... or is it John you're after?

Christine I've told you I don't want to marry you. And that's final.

Katie enters

Katie Oh, here you are. Hello, Dominic.

Dominic Go off and play, Katie.
Katie No.
Dominic What?
Katie No, I've had enough. Me bum's all wet with falling down.
Christine Would you like a hot tatie for the walk home?
Katie Oh, yes, please.
Dominic Christine ...
Christine Do you want one, Dominic?
Dominic No!

He goes

Katie See you later, Dominic.
Christine (*laughing*) Katie O'Brien, you little devil!
Katie Did I do something wrong?

David Bracken enters behind during the next and waits for Christine

Christine My little guardian angel. For that performance I think you deserve two taties. Come on, I'd better get you home before your bottom turns to ice.

They start to go

Katie I'm not really wet, you know, but it's all I could think of.

Christine takes Katie and David by the hand and exits

The singing swells. The Lights change, the bonfire goes. The singing is now located on the R side and very faint till it disappears as the following scene starts

As this is happening, John and Mary walk slowly in from L

The music fades. An awkward silence. (They have walked in silence for nearly an hour)

Mary John, for God's sake. Say something, please!

He pulls her to him and kisses her. They break. There is a pause

John Mary ... I ...
Mary Well, thank heavens for that. For a minute there I was beginning to think you'd lost the power of speech.
John (*laughing*) Well, I didn't know ... well, you——

She laughs

—you didn't say anything either ... Oh, you know what I mean.
Mary Yes. Well, now you've finally declared your intentions, Mr O'Brien, would you care for a repeat performance?
John (*laughing and kissing her, then breaking*) Hey, there's no-one about, is there?
Mary Does it matter? (*She kisses him*)

He laughs

What's so funny?

John It's just ... this, us, you and me, like a couple of kids up the lane. Somehow I can't quite believe it.

Mary I can. Just. (*She laughs*) Surprising, isn't it?

John Ay. But nice mind. (*He kisses her*) You know, I had sort of made up my mind not to see you again.

Mary (*smiling*) And now?

John I'd have been as miserable as sin if you hadn't been there.

Mary Good. (*She kisses him*) I love you, John.

John (*shaking his head*) The school-teacher and the docker. What'll they say when this gets about?

Mary I don't really care. Do you?

John Are you sure you know what you're letting yourself in for?

Mary I think so.

John Do you think you can stand it? My ma already thinks I'm half-way to the madhouse after the other night. As for yours ...

Mary John, you won't let anything separate us, will you?

John It's me should be saying that to you.

Mary Promise me. Nothing or no-one, ever?

John laughs

What're you laughing for? I mean it!

John (*pulling her to him*) I know. I'm sorry. I can't help it. I can't ... I keep expecting to wake up with me feet sticking out of the bottom of the bed and Dominic snoring in me ear.

Mary For your information, John O'Brien, I don't snore. (*She goes to kiss him*)

John Mary, are you sure about this ... ? I mean, well ... you're ... I'm just a big thick docker and ...

Mary Oh, John, please stop running yourself down. (*She goes to kiss him*)

John No, I am. I know I am, and I'm ashamed of it.

Mary You just think you are, that's all. (*She kisses him and holds him tight*)

John Will you teach me?

Mary John!

John Please. I wouldn't want you to be ashamed of me ...

Mary Don't be stupid, John.

John I suppose you've heard of our family. It isn't that I'm ashamed, only ... well, there's never been much chance for any of us. My ma has slaved all her life and——

Mary Sssh! I love you, that's all that matters now.

They kiss. The Lights change

The Musician enters in the back structure playing

John and Mary exit arm in arm

Young lads enter and strike the snowcloths

As this is happening, we see Nancy Kelly isolated in the back structure, smiling

The Lights change

Father Bailey enters followed by John. They head for the forestage and the setting is somewhere on the waterfront

The music fades and the Lights go down on Nancy

Father Bailey Why America all of a sudden? What's brought this on?

John Well, there's not exactly a lot to keep me here, is there?

Father Bailey Two weeks a gaffer and suddenly it's not good enough? John?

John Ay, well, there's not much else beyond that, is there?

Father Bailey For some, it's their life's ambition.

John Is it a sin to want to better yourself, Father?

Father Bailey Greed can be an evil companion.

John Is poverty a better one?

Father Bailey John, easy now. This is not Father O'Malley you're talking to. I'm only asking. One minute you're cock-a-hoop and the youngest gaffer on the docks, the next you're off to America to make your fortune. I can't help but wonder.

John It's not enough, that's all.

Father Bailey Money doesn't necessarily bring you contentment, John.

John And working on the docks all my life will?

Father Bailey It's enough for a lot of people.

John Look, Father, I happened to be born a docker and I've nothing against your God for that, but I'll be damned if I'll imprison myself on the waterfront for the rest of my life and be buried a docker. And, with respect, Father, I can't for the life of me see why the hell I should.

Father Bailey And America's the answer?

John Maybe. If only half the rumours are true, it'll be a damned sight better than what's in line for me here. I can work as good as the next man and better than most. If the opportunity is there, I'll have a go.

Father Bailey Ambition is a cruel——

John Why shouldn't I be ambitious? I know I can do a lot better than the fifteen streets!

Father Bailey Some don't.

John Ay, well, I'll take my chances. It can't be any worse than what I can see here. Old man Llewellyn, he was on the docks and he worked himself up. If he can, I don't see why I can't.

Father Bailey So ... (*He pauses*)

John So, what?

Father Bailey (*smiling at John*) I don't walk around with my eyes shut, you know, John. Or my ears for that matter. Much as you would like to think I do.

John Ay, well ...
Father Bailey Do you want to talk about it?
John No.
Father Bailey It's not an easy path you're treading, John.
John It's the only way.
Father Bailey Are you sure?

John looks at him

   Both sure?

No reaction

   I'm not going to argue, John. I can see that light in your eye that wasn't
   there a month ago. Believe me when I say I understand——
John You!
Father Bailey (*laughing*) I wasn't born a priest, you know.

John smiles

   Tell me, does your ma know?
John Ay. She thinks I'm off me rocker.
Father Bailey About America?
John No point in fretting her about that. I'm not going yet.
Father Bailey And if you do?
John I'll send money, and when I'm set up they'll come to me.
Father Bailey And Mary?
John I hope so.
Father Bailey Take great care, John.
John I am doing.
Father Bailey I can see that. Ay, and maybe you're right and the world's
   wrong, but I can tell you they won't think so.
John No.
Father Bailey Ay, well, look, no more warnings. All things in their own
   time. I'll write to Old Hogan and ask for details. Come on, let's walk
   back. Oh, and John, promise me next time you want to talk in private, can
   we stay in the church? I'm freezing to death up here!

They start to go

   And another thing, for heaven's sake don't let Father O. hear of this or
   there'll be the Devil to pay, believe you me.

   They go

SCENE 4

*The Musician plays. The Lights change. We see Nancy Kelly isolated in the
back structure, staring out front and grinning*

*At the same time, the O'Brien house rolls forward. Shane, Dominic and Mary
Ellen are in the front room looking across the street at Nancy*

Molly, Mick and Katie rush in

Mary Ellen I've told you! Out! And stay out!

They go

John enters, whistling

No whistling! How many times ... haven't we enough trouble without you whistling?

Shane (*to himself*) The swine should be crucified.

John What's up?

Mary Ellen It's Nancy ... she's going to have a bairn.

Nancy's light goes at the back and she walks off

John What?

Mary Ellen It's true. Hannah's had her to the doctor. She's nearly out of her mind.

John Nancy? Nancy Kelly? God in heaven. But who in their right mind ... ?

Mary Ellen She won't say. She's gone all stubborn, like. She won't do what she's told, just stands around, grinning. Honest, John, you wouldn't believe the change in her. I mean, I can't keep her out of the house. When she's not in here grinning at me, she's over at her front door, staring over here. She's frightened me half to death all day, just walking in without so much as a by-your-leave. It's as if she's proud ... proud of it ... Oh, I dunno.

John How's Joe?

Mary Ellen Hannah hasn't had the strength to tell him. Do you blame her?

Shane This'll send the little bantam clean off his head.

Mary Ellen Shane, I don't want ...

Nancy enters through the front

Look, Nancy, if I've told you once ... get yourself away home!

Nancy (*defiantly*) No. (*She walks into the kitchen, stands looking from one to the other of the men, walks to John, puts her hand on his sleeve*) John?

There is a pause

John (*clearing his throat*) Yes, Nancy?

Nancy (*grinning at him*) John ...

John Yes. What is it, Nancy?

Nancy John ... what are we going to do when the bairn's born?

Dominic bursts out cackling with laughter, pointing at John and Nancy. Shane and Mary Ellen are stunned

John (*to Dominic*) You bloody swine!! (*He goes for Dominic*)

Shane (*holding John back*) No, son. Not in the house!

Dominic (*moving to the back yard, pulling his jacket off*) Come on then! Let him fight, the dirty bastard! Come on then, "God Almighty"! Now I'll give you the lessons!

He goes off

John throws Mary Ellen and Shane aside and follows Dominic

Mary Ellen No! For God's sake, stop them!
Shane (*grabbing her*) No, lass, don't! Let them have it out! It'll be for the best!
Mary Ellen No! No! He'll kill him. John'll kill him.

They go out to the back yard

The Lights change

The Musician enters playing the hurdy-gurdy

The O'Brien truck is rolled back quickly

John and Dominic enter, fighting, and move to the forestage, surrounded by kids shouting

Adults enter and take sides in the fight

Peggy Flaherty enters on her level

Father Bailey is in evidence in the back structure, watching, as are Peter and David Bracken

All Fight! Fight . . . *etc.*
Kids (*chanting*) The O'Briens are fighting . . . *etc.*

The hubbub and shouting are kept up throughout, underneath the music

During this, Christine enters

The fighters part momentarily and she walks between them. Crowd reaction. Mary Ellen closes her eyes. John at the last minute pulls his punch. The crowd reacts with relief

Mary Ellen Oh, my son! What happened?
Shane She stopped them. The lass from next door.
Mary Ellen Thank the Lord.

She moves to John, tries to pull him away. He wants to fight on. Christine is still between them

John (*quietly*) One of these days, I'll kill you.

John moves away with Mary Ellen. Christine turns to Dominic

Dominic This is one time I'm fighting in the right.
Christine Fighting was never in the right.
Dominic No? Huh! (*He spits some blood*) Not even when your wonderful John gives Nancy Kelly a bairn?

The crowd reacts. All freeze

That's right, you heard. John O'Brien put mad Nancy up the stick!

He exits through the crowd

Snap lighting change, isolating the kids who are now in a tight group C, *Father Bailey and Peter Bracken in the back structure (Peter Bracken to be joined by Christine). The adult neighbours and Joe and Nancy Kelly* DL, *the O'Brien family* R, *John* DR. *All focus on John as the kids start chanting*

Kids   John O'Brien kissed her lips
             Now Nancy Kelly's up the stick.
             We know Nancy is quite mad.
             But John O'Brien is the dad!

During the next verse, the kids exit

             John O'Brien kissed mad Nancy,
             Gave her money, tickled her fancy.
             We know Nancy is quite mad,
             But John O'Brien is the dad.

They exit R, *still singing*

The music, which has been insistent, rises in tension as they exit until Joe Kelly followed by two or three male adults breaks over to R *and focuses a scene around John. The rest of the isolated pictures remain throughout. The scene is now on the waterfront. Music underpins the scene*

Joe Kelly breaks over to John

Joe Well, what have you got to say for yourself?
John What about?
Joe You know bloody fine what about!
John Joe . . . for Christ's sake, man, have some sense! What do you think I am? Do you really think that I . . . I've always been kind to her . . . for God's sake, Joe, I'm not that hard up for a woman!
Joe Why did you take her up the country then?
John Me?
Joe Ay, and gave her money. You might be a big bastard, O'Brien, but I'm going to kick the guts out of you!
John (*grabbing him and pinning him against the dock wall*) If there's any guts to be kicked out, I can do a bit of that myself, Joe Kelly! But first, get this straight. This whole thing's a pack of damned lies from beginning to end! You bring me the one that saw me up the country with Nancy, or let's get Nancy and ask her. Then we'll see who'll do the kicking! (*He releases Joe*)
Joe All right, then! If you've got the face, O'Brien, come and clear yourself.

Joe leads. John follows. Joe crosses to Hannah. The adults part and form round them. The Lights change

             Get her out here!

A group of kids enter in the back structure and watch

Hannah It's late, Joe!
Joe Get her up!

Hannah brings Nancy through. She is in her nightgown

John Look, Nancy, have I ever taken you up the country?

Nancy looks at him. She is sleepy

   Have I? Have I? Ever?

Nancy No, John.

John Now, have I ever given you money?

Nancy Yes.

John Listen carefully, now. When did I give you the money?

Nancy (*after a pause*) Up Simonside.

Joe Simonside is the country.

Nancy Yes.

Joe Want to know any more?

John Yes! Nancy, how much did I give you?

Nancy Threepence.

John And what did I give it you for?

Nancy For being a good girl.

Joe You——

John I know the night I gave it to her. I met her crying under the arches. Annie had left her in the market and she hadn't her tram fare. She was afraid to stand outside the bar and I put her on the tram and ... Bella Bradley was on that tram. It was her who put this into your head.

Joe She said she saw you coming down the Simonside bank with her.

John How the hell could she if she was in the tram and it black dark?

Joe has no answer to this. He looks from John to Nancy

Joe (*pointing at John*) Has he ever touched you?

Hannah Joe ...

Joe Answer me. Has he? (*He grabs her and tries to shake out the answer*) Did he touch you? You know what I mean. Come on, answer me. Did he put his hands in your clothes like you know men shouldn't?

Hannah For God's sake ...

Joe Stay out of this! Come on, answer me! Did you lie down for him? Did he pay you to let him play with you? Answer! You slut! Did he? (*He makes to hit her*)

Hannah (*pulling at Joe*) Leave her be, man!

Nancy (*breaking free, shouting at Joe*) Leave me alone ... see you! You hit me if you dare, see! I'm gonna have a bairn, I am ... an' be married ... yes, I am. I'm gonna be married when the bairn's born, I am. (*She's pulling at her nightgown*) Aren't I, John? (*She smiles at John, moves towards him*) John?

John (*shouting*) Take your hands off me! (*He breaks away to the dock area*)

Joe You won't get away with it like that! You filthy bastard! (*He hits Nancy*) You stupid little whore! Get out of my sight, you slut! I wish you'd never been born, you simple, stupid bitch!

He pushes her off, still hitting her

Hannah Joe, don't!

Snap lighting change, isolating John DR, adult neighbours DL, the O'Brien family RC, *Father Bailey in the back structure, Peter, Christine and David Bracken in back structure, the Musician, the group of kids in the back structure. With the Lights the kids chant the verse "John O'Brien kissed her lips". They chant this to John, and repeat throughout the following until the next scene is set*

> *During the above, the adults who are all focused on John leave the stage. There should be little doubt in the neighbours' minds that he is guilty. The last to leave are the O'Brien family who are pretty shell-shocked at what has happened. The last of those to leave is Katie*

> *As Katie leaves, the maids and footmen, etc. enter and set up the Llewellyn house, then leave*

The kids still repeat their chant throughout to John, isolated in light DR *on the forestage. When the furniture is set, the Lights change*

> *The kids exit, still singing*

The music stops

John remains in the dock area throughout the following. He is reading a letter

SCENE 5

The Lights rise on the Llewellyns' drawing-room. Beatrice and Mary are there

Mary You sent for me?
Beatrice It seems I have to these days.
Mary You wanted to see me.
Beatrice From now on, Mary, you will conform to the rules of this house. If it is your intention to stay in it, that is?

Silence

> Our meals are served in the dining-room! If you do not deign to have them with us, then I'm afraid you'll have to eat out for I shall no longer have them taken to your room.

Mary Will that be all?
Beatrice No! Are you in such a hurry to see your docker? Don't think I don't know where you slink off to every night. Well, I'm not having my servants embroiled in your sordid little intrigues. Deliver your own shameful letters in future, please.

Mary makes to go

> Are you so infatuated with your docker that you must write to him as well?

Mary Yes!
Beatrice Oh, Mary ... even the servants are laughing at you. Can't you hear them giggling in corners?
Mary I hear them!

Beatrice Have you no shame?

Mary No! I have nothing to be ashamed of, except your ... And for your information, I haven't seen John all week, so tell your spies they'd better sharpen up!

Beatrice My God, Mary, is that why you were at the dock gates this afternoon? Is it?

Silence

Like a whore ... a common whore!

Mary Yes! Like a whore! If you care to put it like that! I love him. I wanted to see him. Needed to. It was the only way, and I would have if it hadn't been for your accidentally turning up. He's the finest man I have ever met. And I'll go on waiting! Yes, outside the dock gates if necessary! There's a reason for his avoidance. You could see that tonight if you'd cared to look. Now, will you please get it into your filthy bigoted mind that I love him! Nothing will keep me from seeing him. Not you, Father, or any humiliation I have to suffer. I don't care! He's a fine man and he loves me. I will not lose him because of any petty little prejudices, not from his people or mine. Now leave me alone!

Beatrice (*quietly*) He's the father of an imbecile girl's child. Did he tell you that?

There is a pause as Mary takes in what has been said

Mary What? What did you say?

Beatrice You heard what I said.

Mary And you expect me to believe you?

Beatrice No. All Tyneside could believe it, but not you. You are so obsessed by that ... that man, that individual with the brutalized, battered face, whose licentiousness drives him to take a poor imbecile——

Mary Be quiet! How dare you! Damn you!

Beatrice Don't you dare speak to me like that!

Mary I will! You sit there taking a man's character away ... damning him ... you ... you know nothing ...

Beatrice His character?

Mary You don't even know him.

Beatrice Can a man have any character who would touch that dreadful Kelly girl?

Mary Kelly? You mean Nancy Kelly?

Beatrice Yes, I mean Nancy Kelly.

Mary You're mad.

Beatrice Am I ... ?

Mary No man would ... would go with that girl.

Beatrice She's going to have a child, and you don't for a moment imagine it's an Immaculate Conception, do you? (*She smiles*) His exalted position of being a gaffer is in jeopardy, too, I understand. For even certain dock men have standards of morals.

Mary (*trying to control her anger*) Yes, for your sake, I should hope so, seeing that my father worked in the docks until he was twenty. You seem

to forget that, don't you? I, in my way, am doing exactly what you did . . .
taking up with a dock worker.

Beatrice (*rising, fuming*) There's a coarseness in you, Mary, that disgusts
me! Your father was never a dock worker. He was apprenticed to a trade,
as well you know.

She storms off

Mary What difference does that make?

The Lights change, isolating Mary C. *Music*

A servant enters and hands her her coat and shawl, then exits

Mary puts them on

At the same time, a Light isolates John DR, *reading a letter*

*Also evident is Nancy Kelly in the back structure grinning but not focused on
the action. She will remain in evidence throughout the following scene*

As this happens, the Llewellyn drawing-room is struck

SCENE 6

Mary moves DL *as John folds the letter and stands. She is isolated in a Light
and is now in the meeting place waiting for him. As John speaks, the Lights
change and the setting is the country at night at their meeting place*

John moves across. Mary does not see him

John Mary . . .
Mary Oh! John?
John Yes. I'm sorry. I didn't mean to frighten you.
Mary It doesn't matter. You're here . . .
John Mary, if I had enough money, would you marry me?
Mary We don't need money, John. I——
John Would you marry me?
Mary Yes, yes, you know I would.

They embrace

John Do you love me enough to wait a year, perhaps two?
Mary John, why?
John Do you?
Mary Yes, but——
John I'm going off to America.
Mary John, you can't!
John I'm going as soon as I can. I went up to see some people called Hogan
in Jarrow last night. They've told me what to do. They've family over
there.

Mary John, stop this. Now, listen to me. Now, don't get wild at what I'm going to say. I've got a little money . . .

He tries to pull away

Now, don't be foolish. It's not a lot! It's what my grandfather left me. We could go together.

John No! I've got to go. Will you wait?

Mary Please, John . . .

John Will you?

Mary (*sighing*) Yes. Yes, I'll wait.

John Good. (*He looks at her*) Mary, I . . .

Mary It's this Nancy Kelly business, isn't it?

John (*after a pause*) You know?

Mary Yes.

John (*after a pause*) You know what it is they're saying?

Mary Yes. Mother took great delight in telling me not two hours ago.

John (*angrily*) She's got the whole bloody town shouting about it, then?

Mary John, it's nonsense. Anyone who knows you couldn't believe——

John They do, but they believe it, all of them, talking and whispering and staring. They point me out on the street, and the kids . . . she . . . I can't prove I'm innocent! I can't! I tried and she . . . Oh, Christ, Mary . . . ! (*Quietly*) I am innocent, Mary.

Mary I know.

John (*embracing her*) I've always been sorry for the girl. I used to mind her when she was a bairn, and she'd come to me when she was frightened. I can't understand it. For some reason, she's made a dead set for me with this thing, and I can't shake it off. They believe her. It's all over town, even your mother . . . oh, Mary, I'm sorry.

Mary I love you. (*She kisses him*)

John I need you, Mary. (*After a pause*) Did you mean what you said? You'll come with me?

Mary Yes.

He kisses her

John (*holding her*) I'll make money, Mary, I promise. We'll start together, just you and me, and we'll be rid of this . . . this shitheap forever!

Mary Yes.

She kisses him. The Lights change and the Musician plays

   They exit

SCENE 7

We see Nancy isolated in the back structure looking out. She will remain isolated like this throughout the next scene

The O'Brien truck rolls forward. Mary Ellen is in the front room staring across the street (at Nancy). Dominic is washing his feet in the kitchen

The Lights come up on the O'Brien truck

Mary Ellen (*to herself*) Lying, dirty slut! My God, how can they think that our John would ever lay his hands on you, you dirty little scrubber. I swear, I swear if he leaves us, I'll be over there with the poker and splatter what little brain you have left all over the flags. I swear it, so help me. You ... you ... (*She stops herself, pinches her nose to stop herself crying, enters the kitchen*)
Dominic She still there?
Mary Ellen Lying little bitch! What does she want with us?
Dominic John?
Mary Ellen Why can't you wash your feet in the scullery like the others? You'd never see our John doing that.
Dominic (*sarcastically*) No! Our John gets Nancy to do it for him.

Mary Ellen takes a swipe at Dominic. He ducks and laughs. He starts picking his toes with a pocket-knife. She is upset and goes to the bedroom, checks she's alone, kneels and a little self-consciously, prays

Mary Ellen Almighty God ... Almighty ... Great and Almighty God ... Ruler of our lives. You who can do all things, grant me this one prayer and I swear unto You that never, until the day I die, will I miss Mass. Please don't let my lad go to America ... please help me do something, make something happen to stop him. Only you can do this ...
Katie (*off*) Ma! Ma!

She enters, sees Dominic in the kitchen and stays in the scullery

Ma! Ma! I want you!
Mary Ellen (*entering the scullery*) What is it, hinny?
Katie Sssh! (*Pointing to the kitchen, whispering*) I'm off to the slipway with Christine.
Mary Ellen What for?
Katie The boat's there.
Mary Ellen Boat?
Katie David's boat. For rowing in. His granda' bought him it for Christmas. Remember, I told you.
Mary Ellen How could I forget. It's too windy, hinny. You'll get blown off the wall.
Katie I won't be on the wall, Ma. The boat won't be on the wall. (*She laughs*) It'll be in the water.
Mary Ellen Who'll be there?
Katie Christine and David. Christine knows all about boats ... she can row! Anyway, Ma, it's tied up, and Christine says it's too windy to go out in it the day. She said maybe tomorrow if the wind goes down we'll have a sail ... there's a sail too, Ma!
Mary Ellen Is there now? (*She laughs, takes a comb from her pinny and combs Katie's hair*)
Katie Ma, Christine's waiting ...

Mary Ellen bends down and holds Katie tight and kisses her. Katie looks at her mother, then returns the kiss

Mary Ellen There, there. That's enough of that. Off you go, then.
Katie (*as she goes*) 'Bye, Ma!

Katie exits

Mary Ellen And mind you're not late for your tea! (*She smiles and goes into the kitchen*)

Dominic enters from the front room, pulling on his outdoor clothes, and goes past her out the back

Dominic ... (*She starts clearing up Dominic's mess*)

Shane enters

Shane Ignorant, that 'un, lass. Not so much as a "see you later". Nowt. Sometimes I reckon it doesn't matter whether I'm here or not. He been drinkin'?
Mary Ellen What d'ye think?
Shane He's a waster, that 'un, lass. We'd all be a lot better if we could pack him off to America instead of our John.
Mary Ellen Ay.
Shane You'd better get some sleep this afternoon or you'll be ending up as barmy as that piece across the way.
Mary Ellen (*smiling*) Do you want your dinner now or wait for John?
Shane I'll wait.
Mary Ellen How's he doing?
Shane How'd you bloody think with all this hanging over him?

John enters, very strained and sits at the table

Storm's lashing itself out.
Mary Ellen Ay, and about time too.

Mary Ellen puts the dinner out. They eat in silence

Shane We got her out all right, didn't we?

John looks hard at Shane. Mary Ellen is aware of Shane's comment

John You did that.
Shane (*embarrassed*) Oh ey, no need for that, son.

They eat. Mary Ellen wipes a tear

Molly (*off*) Ma! Ma! Ma! Ma!
Mary Ellen I'll box her lugs for her, screaming like that. What's she think she's playing at?

Molly enters

Molly (*entering; still screaming*) Ma! Ma! Ma! Oh, Ma.
Mary Ellen (*stopping her in the scullery; shouting*) What?
Molly Ma! It's Katie! ... Katie and Christine!
Mary Ellen (*shaking Molly*) What? What is it? What's happened? John!

John and Shane are stunned and take a while to register what's happened

Molly They're in the gut! In the boat . . . it's going round and round down the river. They're in the gut! It was our Dominic. He tried to get in the boat with Christine, and she pushed him back, our Katie loosened the rope . . . I was watching behind the wall. He tried to get in the boat. Oh, Ma. They're going down the gut in the boat . . . they haven't got any oars or nothing. And David's screaming on the slipway. Ma, the boat's going round and round down the river . . .

John and Shane run out

John (*as he runs out*) Make straight for the slacks! They'll be in the main gut by now!

They exit

The Lights change

SCENE 8

The Lights change as the Musician enters playing the hurdy-gurdy

Nancy turns in the back structure and starts shouting "Katie! Katie!" UL. She continues with this until the scene is set

The O'Brien truck moves quickly back

The cast flood the stage as if the river is upstage. They use lots of improvisation to cover the setting up of a truck which looks like a set of harbour steps and gives access down from the back structure to the stage. The Lights change. As soon as this is set the rest of the cast fill the steps all facing and shouting upstage. They are concentrated and lit in a very small space as opposed to trying to fill the stage

Crowd (*variously*) There they are! Oh God, they've no chance. Can you see them? What's happening? What is it? . . . etc.

John enters at stage level followed by Shane. They fight their way up through the crowd into the back structure

John Where are they? Let me through. Get out of my bloody way, will you?

John throws one of the onlookers to the ground. He goes to fight back. Shane pushes him away

Shane She's our kid. My daughter. Get away. Let him through, for Christ's sake!

They both shove people out of the way as they fight to the front

Molly and Mary Ellen enter and push to the front

John reaches the front as the crowd gasps

John Where are they? Where? Where?

Crowd (*variously*) They've gone. This minute. You're too late. . . . *etc.*

John (*shouting*) No . . . Katie? Christine. Katie. Where were they? Where? Tell me. Where?

Crowd (*variously*) There. There. Over there. No, there.

John Where? Point, can't you?

Hannah There they are! There. There. They're alive. Look.

Snap lighting change. The crowd all turn the same way to face front and focus on the boat in the auditorium L. This is held for an instant before they all start breaking from the back structure and down on to the forestage. The Lights change. The auditorium is now the gut. John remains isolated. The tempo of music changes. There is a deep swirling water effect in the auditorium which plays until the end of this scene

John, still at the back, screams out to the boat in the auditorium

John Katie! Hold the sides of the boat! Hold on! Stay still! Don't stand up! Christine! Christine! (*He moves along the back structure till he is above the crowd but not at stage level*) Katie! Sit down! Christine! Tell her to sit down! Christine! Katie! Hold on I'm coming! (*He drops into the crowd from the back structure*) Katie! Hold the sides of the boat! Hold the sides! Good . . . good girl! (*The boat starts to move R to the centre of the auditorium. John moves with it still shouting*) Don't move! It'll be all right! (*He looks back at the crowd and dives in and grabs a pole off one of the bystanders*) Christine! Katie! Over there! (*He moves to DR on the forestage*)

The rest of the crowd remain focused on the boat. John shouts out to the boat

Christine! Katie! When you pass grab the pole! Christine! Oh for God's sake, Christine!

Throughout the above he has been unable to get any reaction whatsoever from Christine. By now John is isolated R, the crowd L

When you pass! When you pass . . . grab the——

A huge gasp from the crowd. The music stops. Silence. The sound of the water laps the auditorium gently. The boat has turned over at the back of the auditorium

Noooo! (*Possible echo effect enhances the emptiness on this*) No! No! (*He throws the pole down, moves back to take off his jacket and is going to dive into the river*)

He is stopped by a couple of bystanders who break from the crowd and bring him down roughly and hold him down, as John is still shouting for Katie

Peter (*grabbing hold of John's hair*) They've gone. It's no use! Don't make another. John . . . John . . .

John is suppressed by the men and reacts to Peter Bracken's plea. Silence. All look and focus to where the boat went down. All are well devastated by this tragedy

David who has remained in the dock area L *calls out to the boat. The Lights isolate him*

David Christine! I want Christine! I want my sister.

The crowd focus on the boy. Silence

John Dominic!

The Musician hits one stroke on the boran. He will underscore the next two scenes with this instrument

The Lights snap up on Dominic somewhere in the back structure L

(*Shouting to him*) Dominic! (*He goes for him through the crowd*)

They try to stop him

Peggy Don't lad, he's not worth it. What's done's done!
John (*trying to push through them*) Let me through!
Hannah Think of your mother, lad.
Bella Lad, it's done.
Hannah You can't bring them back, John.
John Dominic!

He bolts back into the back structure R *to gain access to Dominic. Dominic tries to escape* R, *can't because of John. He exits* L. *John follows*

The kids exit after them with cries of "Fight! Fight!"

Throughout the above the O'Brien family have remained focused on the boat in the auditorium. Peter Bracken has crossed to David L *and is consoling him. The Musician strikes a dominant beat on the boran as Father Bailey drags Shane away. Peggy Flaherty takes Mick away. The women usher out Mary Ellen. Peter and David Bracken leave. Nancy takes Molly's arm and takes her away. Molly is in floods of tears*

The Lights and the tempo of music change

SCENE 9

The stackyard is set up quickly. This consists of three large stacks of timber. One emerges from L, *another from* R, *and the harbour steps convert into the third—they form three stacks of timber about six to eight feet high with a "T" passageway between them*

During this change, John is in evidence in the back structure looking for Dominic

When the stacks are set the Lights change and the drum changes tempo. We are now in the stackyard with John on the UC *stack, Dominic hiding at stage level. John hears Dominic. He jumps from the* UC *to the* DR *stack. Dominic hears him but cannot see him. He is about to go. John jumps down from the stack and confronts him. Dominic tries to bolt. John grabs him*

Molly enters up the back

Molly (*screaming*) Ma!!!!

The rest of the cast save Mary Ellen and Shane enter

There follows a very savage and brutal fight in which John is very definitely trying to kill Dominic. (NB. Queensberry rules do not apply and the fight should be as shocking as it is exciting, both parties being very brutal combatants.) The crowd and kids all improvise their way through this, making a lot of noise and getting involved in the action. Eventually Dominic is battered unconscious and is thrown DC. John goes for him again and is dragged off by some of the crowd and suppressed. The women crowd Dominic

Peggy My God! Leave him be, lad! He's had enough!
Hannah God almighty! I think he's done for him.
Peggy Oh, Jesus have mercy on us, he's killed him.
Bella God almighty! It'll be a hanging job!
Hannah Ay, heaven help us! It'll be a hanging job!

Mary Ellen enters

They move to Mary Ellen. She is standing away from them

You can do no good here, Mary Ellen.
Peggy You must think of yourself and Shane.
Hannah Ay, Shane's lying back here, bad. The shock's been too much for him . . .
Peggy Ay, come on, lass.
Bella We'd best take her out of this. There's nothing she can do now.
Hannah Come on, lass.
Bella Is she all right? Mary Ellen?
Hannah Mary . . .

Mary Ellen has not reacted but she wants to scream. Nancy screams. The women turn. Nancy is kneeling next to Dominic

Nancy Dominic! Dominic! Don't be dead! I've kept my mouth shut, Dominic . . . I did what you told me. I kept quiet . . . don't be dead . . . you must marry me when the bairn's born . . . I've been a good girl, Dominic. I did what you told me. Dominic? Dominic?

Nancy is shaking Dominic. John pushes her aside and grabs Dominic and is going to kill him

John You . . . you filthy lying . . . ! (*He is about to hit him*)

The men grab hold of him and suppress him

I'll kill you. I'll kill you. I'll kill you.

The men suppress John. Joe Kelly breaks towards Dominic. Hannah breaks from the women and stops him

Hannah No, Joe!

Peggy (*to two of the men*) You! And you. Look slippy there! (*She refers to Dominic*) Get him out of here!

The women galvanize into action and usher the men carrying Dominic away L

Father Bailey goes to follow but Peggy prevents him

Joe Kelly ushers Father Bailey away R

Most of the others leave

The men release John. He makes to go after Dominic. Mary Ellen steps in front of him

John I'll find him.

Mary Ellen turns and walks off

The men follow, keeping an eye on John

I'll find him.

The Lights change. Drumbeats

John goes

The stackyard is cleared

As the stackyard is cleared, the kids appear in the back structure singing

Kids   The O'Briens are fighting
                  First there were five.
                  Now there's only three and a half,
                  'Cos Dominic's just alive.

During the following chant they use sticks to beat out a persistent rhythm

At one point, John is seen working his way through the back structure looking for Dominic

                  John is hunting Dominic.
                  Dominic's on the run
                  If he ever finds him,
                  John's gonna be hung.

As the kids sing, the O'Brien truck rolls forward. They sing the last verse until the Lights come up on the O'Brien house, then exit

SCENE 10

The Lights come up on the O'Brien truck

Shane is in bed in the front room. Molly is standing by him. She has on her mother's pinny. Mary Ellen is in the kitchen, sitting tense, tired and in a state of shock

Molly (*coming through*) Ma, Da won't eat the soup I made. Ma? Would you like some, Ma? (*She sighs, picks two cups of tea off the table*) Ma, which one of these has the pills in? Ma?

Peggy (*off*) He's not going to let him get away with it are you, John?

Molly Oh, my God, they're here. (*She quickly puts the mugs on the table*)

Father O'Malley enters, followed by Peggy and John. John hasn't slept for three days

Peggy He won't give up, Father, not till he finds him. I kept on telling him——

Father O'Malley Be quiet, will you, woman!

Peggy He won't be happy till he finds him . . .

Father O'Malley I'm ashamed of you, Peggy Flaherty. There's not a house in the fifteen streets that's not in turmoil because of you two.

Peggy It was the obvious place to look, Father.

Father O'Malley Enough! The two of you have turned the streets upside down these past three days, but now it's got to stop. Child, give John his tea.

Molly Yes, Father.

Molly gives a mug to John and Father O'Malley. They drink during the following

Peggy We'll find him, John, never fear.

Father O'Malley Mrs Flaherty! Drink up, John.

Peggy (*taking Molly out of the kitchen into the scullery*) That's it, hinny, you be your mother's right hand now. (*Whispering*) How is she?

Molly The same. She's said nowt all day. It's been three days Peggy and she just keeps on mumbling, it's all her fault.

Peggy Ay well, it's a good job you're here in charge, eh? I'm away upstairs now. If you need any help when John's had those sleeping pills, just knock up. (*To John as she re-enters the kitchen*) Justice will be done, John, lad. We'll see to that.

Father O'Malley Out!

Peggy goes

Now, John, I'm telling you. This has got to stop! Who are you to take God's work into your own hands? This senseless pursuit of Dominic must end. The Lord will seek vengeance without your help. Or do you want to be hanged for his death, is that it? John? Leave it now. There's not a room in the fifteen streets you've not pulled apart, now is there? It's God's will, John O'Brien. All you're doing is causing misery. Look at the state of you! He has shown you already what happens when you go against His holy will. I cannot repeat it too often, if you'd kept that man Bracken from your house, this state of affairs would never have come about. (*He yawns*) O'Brien, you've been Godless for years! The ignoring of His holy Mass Sunday after Sunday brings its tribulation . . . (*From now on the sleeping drug begins to get a grip*) Throw off these undesirable . . . companions and come to Mass . . . (*He is very drowsy*)

Mary Ellen turns to look at him

The Lord looks after His own. If you serve Him in humility ... pride ...
pride ... John ... is a terrible ... terrible ... sin ...

*Mary Ellen rises and stares at the priest. He shakes his head, clicks that
something is happening*

What in God's name ... ? Holy Mother ... the Flanagans ... the child
suspected of the sleeping sickness ... I was there ... in the name of God
... no! No! Not me ... no ... not the sleeping sickness ... no ...

Father O'Malley rises. Mary Ellen watches him uncomprehendingly

Molly Father ...

During the following, Father O'Malley staggers out the front

Father O'Malley Out of my way ... Please, Lord, not me ... I'm your
faithful servant ... these people, they ... ignorant! All of them ... they
only know you through fear ... please, God, not me ...

Father O'Malley staggers out the front

*Mary Ellen starts laughing; this reaches an hysterical pitch during the
following*

John Ma! Stop! Stop it! (*Shaking her*) Ma! Stop, be quiet!
Mary Ellen The pills ... the pills ... she put them in the wrong cup ...
John (*shouting*) Ma! Stop it, I tell you!
Shane (*from the bed*) What is it? Why are you laughing? For God's sake!

Mary Ellen's laughter subsides. Her grief surfaces

Mary Ellen Oh, me bairn! Me bonny bairn ... me bonny, bonny bairn ...
John (*it rises in him too as he sees her crumble*) Ma ...

*He holds her. They cry together. The Lights isolate them. The Musician plays
and the O'Brien truck is rolled back. The Lights change*

Scene 11

Father Bailey enters ushering Molly. She runs across the stage

Father Bailey And not a word to a living soul, mind you!
Molly (*calling back as she runs off*) No fear, Father!

She runs off

Peter Bracken enters behind Father Bailey

Father Bailey (*bursting out laughing to himself, unaware of Peter*)
Well, well, well what a turn up. How the mighty are fallen. If I hadn't seen
it with me own eyes I'd have thought the girl was insane. Father O'Malley
of all the——(*He sees Peter, stops laughing*) I'm sorry.

Peter It was as far as I could manage. I couldn't leave him lying on my doorstep.

Father Bailey No, indeed. That would never do not at all, not at all ... would it be putting you out if he stayed?

Peter No.

Father Bailey Then I think we'll leave him to sleep it off on your kitchen floor. (*He chuckles*) He seemed quite comfortable. I promise I'll be there when he wakes up. Oh, yes, I'll be there.

Peter Thank you. It would be appreciated.

Father Bailey Indeed.

Peter The tablets were meant for John. Arrangements have been made to get ... the other one away on to a ship within the hour.

Father Bailey Dominic?

Peter nods

I see. And where is he, might I ask?

Peter (*thinking*) Peggy Flaherty's.

Father Bailey Peggy ... well bless me and her ... of course, of course ... I must be losing my touch.

Peter If John comes to his senses, he'll surely guess. It's the only house he's not searched.

Father Bailey Is Dominic fit enough to work his passage?

Peter No, but that's been taken care of and we can't hide him any longer and there may not be another chance for days.

Father Bailey I see. Can I be of help?

Peter Yes. I have two more tablets. John wouldn't suspect you.

Father Bailey I'll fix the lad. He won't get in your way.

Peter Thank you. (*He gives him the tablets*)

Father Bailey You're a brave and forgiving man, Mr Bracken.

Peter (*with great force*) I am not brave.

Father Bailey But Christine ...

Peter I am not brave. I'm only doing what I must. I don't feel it's John's destiny to die for the likes of ... there are other things for John. He has begun to think. Nothing must stop that ... you see, I know ... Christine has told me, she says——

Father Bailey Christine?

Peter Yes ... that's why I can bear my sorrow easier than the others ... To you death is a parting that only death can join again. To me ... Christine is with me always. But I'm no braver than the next man. I shall miss her dearly. (*He is choked, not looking at Father Bailey*)

Father Bailey Mr Bracken. (*He holds out his hand*) Thank you.

Peter (*shaking it*) You're a brave man yourself, Father.

Father Bailey Hmmm. Look, maybe when this is over, we could talk.

Peter Yes, we could talk. Thank you. But please, we must hurry. If we don't get him on that ship tonight there'll be no time to find another.

They go

The Lights change. The Musician re-establishes the boran and continues to underscore the following scene until John leaves the stage

SCENE 12

Hannah Kelly enters L, *looks around, signals* L. *Peggy enters followed by the other women and girls. Molly is in evidence. Peggy is ushering four men carrying the stretcher. (Mick maybe helping.) Dominic is on the stretcher, heavily bandaged*

Peggy Sssh! Do you want the whole town out to send him off?
Hannah Sssh! Hold your tongue, Peg . . .

Bella enters

Bella Peg?
Peggy Here.
Hannah Sssh!
Bella It's clear this end. Come on.

Mary Ellen bursts in

Peggy
Hannah } (*together*) Whaa!
Bella
Mary Ellen John's coming. The Father couldn't hold him. He's running round the front.
Peggy Holy Mother . . . (*To the men*) Quick hide him over there . . .

They move. She changes her mind

No, no, over there . . .

They move. She changes her mind again

No, no, not there. Over there.

They hide

Bella (*to Mary Ellen*) I thought you——
Mary Ellen He's had the tablets, but he heard you above.
Hannah (*to Peggy*) I told you . . .
Mary Ellen Father Bailey tried to stop him. He managed to stop him coming straight out the back, but he's running round the front.

John enters

The women all take a strong stance together to guard the stretcher and stop John. John is fighting the effect of the tablets until they finally defeat him

Father Bailey enters, heavily out of breath

Father Bailey John . . . John . . . stop. This is for your own good, believe——
John Where is he?
Peggy And who is it you're wanting?
John Don't! Don't play . . . you sneaky bitch!
Bella Oh, very nice . . .
Hannah Well, we can't even take the night air without——
John Where is he? (*He moves to go through them*)

Father Bailey (*stepping in front of John*) John, now enough's enough! Stop
  this.
John Get by!
Father Bailey No, I'm not going to get by. There's nothing you can do. This
  is for your own good. Now get that into that big head of yours. You've
  swallowed a potion that would put a horse to sleep. Now, I'm telling you.

John grabs hold of Father Bailey and throws him aside

John Out of my way!
Mary Ellen (*stepping in front of him*) He's gone, lad.
John No . . . you're lying . . . all of you. (*To Peggy*) You? You . . . no! No!

*John pushes them aside to go up to Peggy's, from this point on Mary Ellen
stays still*

Father Bailey (*following*) John!
Bella Now, quick, move!
Peggy No, stay. He'll be back.
Bella Peggy! He'll kill him, drugged or not!
Peggy Shut your mouth!
Bella That's bloody it! I'm——

John tears in, desperate now. The drug is taking hold

John Where is he? Where . . . where have you . . . I'll find him! I'm telling
  you . . . where . . . Ma? Ma? Ma! . . . Katie . . . Katie, Ma! (*To Hannah*)
  Nancy . . . he . . . where is he, for Christ's sake?
Hannah (*grabbing him*) Stop it . . . d'ye think we wouldn't rather have him
  dead? We would . . . I would. John, stop this . . . Jesus Christ, I'd kill him
  myself! Don't think I couldn't. But I'm not going to die for that bastard!
  I'm not, and you're not! Now get that into your thick head, O'Brien! I
  won't . . . we won't . . . (*She starts to cry*)

*Peter Bracken enters cautiously. He has been awaiting Dominic's arrival.
He watches*

Bella (*comforting Hannah*) Come on, lass. If he wants to swing, let him.
John Ma . . . ? (*He tries to walk away and then slumps*) I'll find him . . .
Peggy (*signalling to the men*) Right . . . keep your eye on him, Father.

*The men come out of the shadows and cross. John sees Dominic. One last
effort*

John Dominic! Dominic . . .

*John tries to rise but fails. The men stop. Dominic raises himself, sees John and
laughs. Peggy shoves him down, roughly*

Peggy Get him out of here! (*She grabs Dominic*) And don't you dare set foot
  in the fifteen streets again . . . you . . . you . . . nasty little bugger! (*She
  throws him down*)

The men take him off, ushered by Peter Bracken

Father Bailey (*picking John up*) It's for the best, lad. Bella, give us a hand here, will you.

She does so. They take John off

Mary Ellen is crying to herself. The Lights change, isolating Mary Ellen and Peggy in the background

Peggy (*quietly*) Come on, lass. It's over now. It's done. Come on.

Mary Ellen Ay ... (*She wipes her face*) Ay ... it's all over. (*She turns to Peggy*) Ay ...

Peggy comforts her as they go

The Lights change

SCENE 13

The Musician plays

The Lights come up and Mary Llewellyn is there. She is waiting for John

John enters to her. He is in his working clothes. He stands looking at her

She senses him there

Mary (*quietly*) John. I knew you'd come eventually. (*She moves to him*) John ... (*She embraces him*)

John (*not responding*) Hello, Mary.

Mary How are you?

John All right.

Mary Your mother?

John All right.

Mary I've missed you, John.

John You came to the house.

Mary I had to. It's been three weeks. You didn't answer my letters.

John No.

Mary Molly said you were out.

John Yes.

Mary Still, you're here now. I knew you'd come. Every night I waite—— I knew ... shall we go up the lane?

John No. (*He moves away from her*)

Mary Talk to me, John. Tell me about it.

John No. Talking won't change anything. It's done ... I'm not going away now. All that business is finished. This business has put paid to my father. He'll never work again. Molly and Mick are still at school ... (*He looks at her*) Nothing can come of it now ... you understand?

Mary No, I don't.

John It's no good going on.

Mary No!

John There's no money coming in, only mine.

Mary We could wait . . . you asked me to wait while you were in America.
John There's nothing to wait for, now.
Mary Molly leaves school in the summer. Your brother will soon be fourteen.
John And what about Ma and Da?
Mary We could always manage to keep them.
John (*angry*) On what? Where would we live? Go on, tell me!

No answer

I'm sorry.
Mary John, look at me.

He does so

We love each other. Don't look away. We do. There won't be anyone else for us. We know that. So, please, don't let this happen. There is a way out.
John There isn't!
Mary There is. There's a way out of everything.
John You sound like old man Bracken.
Mary He's right. It's true.
John No . . .
Mary Listen! If you'll only listen to me. I don't care where I live as long as I'm with you. We could be married and I'd go on working. I'll come to the fifteen streets and——
John (*fuming*) Have you ever been in a house in the fifteen streets? Eh?
Mary There's no disgrace in being poor.
John How would you know? You'll never come to the fifteen streets through me.
Mary John, listen . . .
John No. It's all I've got, do you understand? All I've got and all I ever will have!
Mary John, please . . .
John No! I've got to go. (*He moves to go*)
Mary Don't . . . don't go like this . . . John, I love you!
John Mary. It's over. It's got to finish, right now. All the talking in the world won't make it any different. You'll forget . . .
Mary I won't. How could I? I'll never . . . there will never be anyone else, John. Ever. John, please, please try to find a way out . . . please? (*After a pause*) Katie would have wanted it. She loved to think that we——
John Don't . . . Goodbye, Mary.

He goes

She is devastated. She goes

The music and Lights change

SCENE 14

The Musician plays

Peggy enters on her level

Father O'Malley is in the back structure, Hannah Kelly and the others DR, *Molly and Mick watching* UL, *all isolated in lights. All are watching Peter and David Bracken leave*

Peter and David Bracken enter, carrying their suitcases. They are followed by the group of kids

Kids (*quietly*) Spooky . . . Spooky . . .

Peter Bracken stops. The kids stop. Silence. He walks to a light C

(*Following him*) Spooky . . . Spooky . . .

He stops. They stop

> *Mary Ellen enters, head down. She almost walks into him. She stops, looks at him*

He takes his hat off to her

> *She turns away and ushers Molly and Mick off* L

Peter picks up his bags and starts to move R

> (*Louder than before*) Spooky, Spooky . . .

He stops. They go quiet

> *He pulls himself together and exits* R

> (*Calling after him loudly*) Spooky . . . Spooky . . .

Peggy (*angrily*) Shut your filthy mouths now, you little heathens. Or I'll come amongst you and leather you all so hard you'll not sit down till Christmas!

> *The kids exit in silence. The adults follow*

The music changes tempo and the Lights change

SCENE 15

Music. James Llewellyn is DR *standing, not a happy man. Behind him two men are loading a cart with some of Mary's bits and pieces*

Mary enters holding the statue wrapped in a cloth

Man Is that the lot, Miss?
Mary Yes, that's all.
Man (*looking to James*) Sure, Miss?
Mary Yes, thank you.

Beatrice enters from L. *She has on her outdoor clothes. She stops, looks at Mary*

Beatrice Mary?

Mary looks at her. She looks to James

James?

James says nothing

Beatrice turns and goes

Mary (*to the men*) Are you ready?
James Mary . . .
Mary Yes?

He takes the statue from her

Father.

He puts it on the cart. He goes to take out his wallet

No, Father, please, I can't.
James Oh, lass. (*He hugs her to him*) Remember I'm——
Mary (*to the men*) Ready?
Man Twelve Fadden Street? (*He looks from her to James*)
Mary (*nodding*) Yes.
Man Fadden Street it is then, Miss. (*To the other man*) Come on, move yourself, we haven't got all day.

They push the cart off L

James Goodbye, lass.
Mary Goodbye.

She turns quickly and exits

The music and Lights change

SCENE 16

The O'Brien truck rolls forward. It is now the Brackens' empty house. There is a new brass bed, recently delivered set in the bedroom area. There are two chairs on the kitchen table covered in filthy old dustcloths. There is very little else of note in the house. Some of the basic O'Brien furniture remains covered in old dustcloths

The Lights come up on the empty house

Mary enters L *through the front door* (*NB. The walk through the fifteen streets with the cart has taken great courage but has left its mark*)

The music stops

Mary (*to the men off*) Yes, this is the right place, thank you! In here, all of it!

Mary Ellen enters through the front

Mary Ellen (*to the men*) Stop that, the both of youse! What do you think you're playing at, Miss?
Mary We're going to be neighbours. (*She waves to the men to continue*)
Mary Ellen I'm not blind. I didn't think you were hawking this lot. But you can't.
Katie How is John, Mrs O'Brien?
Mary Ellen Not too grand, but he'll play merry hell when he finds this out.
Mary Do you agree with his decision?
Mary Ellen Look, lass, you don't understand.
Mary Please believe me ... I do understand. I want him to go on looking after you always, but that is no reason why we should be separated, is it, Mrs O'Brien?
Mary Ellen But——
Mary We care for each other very deeply and there is a way out if only he'd listen to reason.
Mary Ellen You can't marry without money, lass.
Mary Did you have money?
Mary Ellen (*shaking her head*) This is different ... you're different. He'd want money to give you a home.
Mary I don't want that kind of home.
Mary Ellen But here, lass? In the streets? Do you know what you're letting yourself in for?
Mary It's the only solution, Mrs O'Brien, for me to come and live here. I must show him I can do it, I can continue my work ... we'll manage.
Mary Ellen What'll people think? What about John? He won't like this, you know.
Mary People can say what they like.
Mary Ellen Does your da know?
Mary (*after a pause*) Yes.
Mary Ellen And what does he think about all this?

No answer

Oh, lass ... (*She doesn't know what to say*)
Mary I'll need your help, Mrs O'Brien. Will you help me? You'll not suffer for it, I promise. Please ... I want to live here. It's just ... will you help me?
Mary Ellen It was the Brackens', you know ... the lass.
Mary Yes, yes, I know ...
Mary Ellen It'll be hard for you ... people ... well, at the very best, it'll be hard going.
Mary You doubt I'll be able to stand it?
Mary Ellen No. Somehow, I don't. If you care for him enough, it'll keep the iron out of your soul.
Mary Thank you. (*She goes to embrace her*)

Mary Ellen Never mind that, lass. You'd best get those blokes moving a storm before our John gets back or there'll be all hell to pay. And we wouldn't want you fighting in the street, not on your first day anyway, eh?

They both laugh. Music. The Lights change

The removal men enter with Mary's bits and pieces in the cart

The two removal men and the women very quickly set up the house. This is a very brisk, efficient, stylized affect. Mary sets up the kitchen table. The men unload the cart. They place the statue (still covered) on the table in the bedroom

The removal men go

Mary Ellen sorts out the bed. She turns, walks to the statue, takes the cloth off it. The Lights come up. The music stops. She is horrified and quickly re-covers the statue. She recognizes the foolishness of this and removes the cloth. Mary Ellen makes her decision and picks the statue up. As Mary moves to the bedroom, Mary Ellen throws the statue to the floor. It shatters

Mary Oh!

Mary Ellen sees her. She is frightened. Pause

Mary Ellen I ... I had to do it, lass ... they would think ... they would think ... the women would say ... they wouldn't understand round these doors ... I ... I wanted you to have a good start.

Mary is still looking at the fragments. The statue was a symbol of her independence

Lass, I didn't mean to hurt you ... (*She is distressed*) I'm sorry ... I didn't ... I don't seem to be able to do anything any——

Mary goes to her and embraces her

Mary There ... there. It's all right. I understand. It was stupid of me. I should have had more sense than to bring it. Please don't cry! Eh, come on. Just think if Father O'Malley had seen it!

She laughs. Mary Ellen joins in

Mary Ellen Eeeh, you'll get by, lass. You'll get by.

Molly rushes in from the back

Molly He's coming up the road, Ma!
Mary Ellen All right. Tell him to come round the front 'cos I'm ... scrubbing the scullery. Go on.

Molly goes out the back

(*To Mary*) Well, lass, I'll get myself away home.

Mary Ellen goes

Mary fusses, but she has run out of time, realizes it

There is a knock L *(as if at next door)*

John *(off)* Ma?

Mary steels herself and goes out

Mary *(off)* John?

Mary enters, John follows. He is in his working clothes. He is stunned. He sees the fragments of the statue, looks at Mary

John Mary . . . *(He shakes his head)* No . . . no, Mary . . . I'm not having this . . . you . . . you can't . . . that's how you'll end, like that, broken.

Mary *(quietly)* Some things are better broken.

John No . . . I won't let you.

Mary You can't stop me . . . I'm here. It's done. Here I am and here I stay until you'll have me. Come and see the kitchen.

She takes his hand and leads him through. The table is set for two. He looks round slowly

Do you like it?

John *(looking at her, then almost to himself)* No . . . no. You don't know what you're doing . . . you'll regret this . . . in time . . . you will. Your father should've——

Mary *(quietly to him and with as much control as she can muster)* Where you go, I shall go . . .

John Mary?

Mary Where you live I shall live. Your people, shall be my people and . . .

John Mary . . .

Mary *(weakly)* Hold me, John.

Pause of some length until John's resolve finally weakens. This decision does not come easy. He crushes her to him and holds her tight

John Mary . . .

He searches her face with his lips, repeating her name. They kiss passionately

The Lights fade. Music

CURTAIN

FURNITURE AND PROPERTY LIST

Only essential props are listed here—please see Production Notes.

ACT I

SCENE 1

No props required

SCENE 2

On stage: Tub of washing for **Hannah**

Off stage: Potty **(Peggy)**
Potty **(Stage Management, Dominic** or **Shane)**

Personal: **Mary Ellen:** pregnancy padding (required until Scene 12)

SCENE 3

On stage: O'Brien truck

Kitchen-cum-parlour:
Table
Chairs, some overturned
Broken picture frame and picture
Dresser/sideboard. *On it:* bread, dripping, plates, cutlery

Scullery:
Box with firewood
Bowl
Bucket of water
Towel, cloth

Front room-cum-bedroom:
Bed with bedding
Small table
Chair

Off stage: Bowl of stew **(Peggy)**
Empty bowl **(Katie)**

Personal: **Dominic:** wages in pocket

SCENE 4

On stage: Hand luggage for **Peter, Christine** and **David Bracken**

SCENE 5

On stage: O'Brien truck

Set: **John**'s coat in front room

SCENE 6

No props required

SCENE 7

Personal: **Catholics:** green ribbons
Protestants: blue ribbons

SCENE 8

On stage: O'Brien truck

SCENE 9

On stage: O'Brien truck

Set: Book for **Katie**
Katie's boots, mending materials and tools for **John**
Shane's coat in scullery

Off stage: Jacket over head **(Dominic)**
Chair **(Peter)**
Blanket and bowl **(Hannah)**
Jug of beer **(Dominic)**
Bag **(Doctor)**

Personal: **Women:** rosaries
John: money

SCENE 10

On stage: Church window

Off stage: Small stool, bell **(Father Bailey)**

SCENE 11

On stage: Sofa
Armchair
Table
Model of yacht
Statue of naked lady
Large draped window

Off stage: Tray with pot of tea, cups, saucers, milk-jug, sugar-bowl **(Maid)**

Personal: **John:** money

SCENE 12

On stage: O'Brien truck

Set: Baking trays, pastry, mincemeat, rolling pin, etc. on kitchen table
              Mince pies, bread, dripping on sideboard
              Knitting in sideboard

Off stage: Gear **(Dominic)**

SCENE 13

On stage: Kitchen section of O'Brien truck

Off stage: Market stalls and produce **(Cast)**
              Parcels **(Mary)**

Personal: **John:** money

SCENE 14

On stage: Kitchen section of O'Brien truck

Off stage: Box with turkey, bag of fruit, holly, chocolates **(John)**

Personal: **John:** comb

ACT II

SCENE 1

On stage: Sofa
              Chairs
              Small table
              Mary's coat

SCENE 2

Off stage: Snowcloths **(Lads)**

SCENE 3

No props required

SCENE 4

On stage: O'Brien truck

Personal: **Dominic:** blood sac in mouth
              John: letter in pocket

SCENE 5

On stage: As Scene 1

Off stage: ' **Mary**'s coat and shawl **(Servant)**

SCENE 6

Personal: **John:** letter

SCENE 7

On stage: O'Brien truck

Set: *Kitchen:*
Bowl of water, towel, pocket knife, socks, shoes
Pots of food on stove, plates

Bedroom:
Dominic's coat

Personal: **Mary Ellen:** comb in apron pocket

SCENE 8

On stage: Truck with harbour steps

Off stage: Pole **(Bystander)**

SCENE 9

On stage: 3 large stacks of timber

Off stage: Sticks **(Kids)**

SCENE 10

On stage: O'Brien truck

Set: 2 cups of tea on kitchen table

SCENE 11

No props required

SCENE 12

On stage: Nil

Off stage: Stretcher **(Men)**

Personal: **Dominic:** bandages

SCENE 13

No props required

SCENE 14

On stage: Nil

Off stage: Suitcases **(Peter, David)**

SCENE 15

On stage: Cart, **Mary**'s bits and pieces

Off stage: Statue wrapped in cloth **(Mary)**

Personal: **James:** wallet

SCENE 16

On stage: O'Brien truck, now the Brackens' empty house

Strike: Most of the furniture
All props

Set: New brass bed in bedroom
2 chairs on table, covered in dustcloths, in kitchen
Dustcloths over other bits of furniture

Off stage: Cart with **Mary**'s bits and pieces, including statue, bedding, crockery, etc.
(Removal Men)

LIGHTING PLOT

Property fittings required: nil

Main set: the O'Brien house—bedroom, kitchen, scullery. Other areas of the stage to represent various simple exterior and interior locations

ACT I

To open: Light on Musician, dim general lighting

Cue 1	As Scene 2 opens *Lighting on each of the groups—***Hannah** DR, *the kids* DL, **Bella**, **Peggy** DL, **Fathers Bailey** *and* **O'Malley** *in back structure* R *and* L	(Page 1)
Cue 2	Kids jeer and run off *Lights isolate* **Bella** *and* **Hannah**	(Page 3)
Cue 3	As Scene 3 opens *Lighting on O'Brien truck*	(Page 3)
Cue 4	**Molly:** "Aw, Ma!" *Lights fade on O'Brien truck*	(Page 9)
Cue 5	When ready for Scene 4 *Lighting on* **Bella**	(Page 9)
Cue 6	**Bella:** "... great van an' all." *Lights up on the* **Brackens** *and the* **O'Briens**, *then lights up on* **Peggy** *and the kids and* **Fathers Bailey** *and* **O'Malley**	(Page 9)
Cue 7	**Dominic** goes off with **Christine** and **David** *Fade lights on* **O'Briens** *and* **Brackens**	(Page 10)
Cue 8	**Bella** drags **Peggy** off *Fade lighing*	(Page 10)
Cue 9	When ready for Scene 5 *Lighting on O'Brien truck*	(Page 11)
Cue 10	**Mary Ellen:** "... about the spooks ... ?" *Fade lighting on O'Brien truck*	(Page 13)
Cue 11	When ready for Scene 6 *Light on* **Musician**, *bring up exterior lighting*	(Page 13)
Cue 12	**Katie** (*off*): "You know I did." *Fade lighting*	(Page 17)
Cue 13	As Scene 7 opens *Bring up lighting on* **Musician** *and Protestants and Catholics*	(Page 17)
Cue 14	**Mary Ellen** drags **Molly** off *Fade lighting*	(Page 17)

Cue 15	When ready for Scene 8	(Page 18)
	Lighting on O'Brien truck	
Cue 16	**Mary Ellen** (*shouting*): "No whistling!"	(Page 19)
	Fade down to lighting on **Mary Ellen**	
Cue 17	**Mary Ellen** crosses herself	(Page 19)
	Fade lights	
Cue 18	As Scene 9 opens	(Page 19)
	Light on **Musician:** *lighting on O'Brien truck*	
Cue 19	**Peter** touches **Christine**'s head and goes	(Page 23)
	Decrease lighting on O'Brien truck; spot on **Musician**	
Cue 20	As **Father O'Malley**, **Brenda Bradley**, **Peggy** and **Nancy** enter	(Page 23)
	Lighting to silhouette the various characters on their various levels; stronger (but still not realistic) lighting to isolate **Mary Ellen** *and* **Christine** *in bedroom;* **John** *and* **Shane** *in kitchen;* **Molly**, **Katie** *and* **Mick** *in scullery;* **Peter Bracken** *on level* L	
Cue 21	As Scene 10 opens	(Page 28)
	Sharp pool of light on **Katie** R; *pool of light on* **John** L	
Cue 22	**Father Bailey** enters and sits C	(Page 28)
	Pool of light C; *fade pool of light on* **John**	
Cue 23	As **Father Bailey** goes	(Page 29)
	Crossfade to pool of light on **John** L	
Cue 24	**Katie:** "... says that if I ..."	(Page 30)
	Fade Light on **John**. *Bring up lighting on Mary's drawing-room*	
Cue 25	**Mary:** "... until Katie is a little older."	(Page 32)
	Fade to half-light on **John** *and* **Mary**; *highlight* **Musician**	
Cue 26	**Mary** stands and walks to the back	(Page 32)
	Return to previous lighting	
Cue 27	**Mary:** "I'll see you out."	(Page 34)
	Crossfade to pool of light on **John** and **Mary** *downstage*	
Cue 28	**John:** "Miss Llewellyn is 'wonderful'." (*He laughs*)	(Page 35)
	Change to exterior lighting	
Cue 29	**John** and **Nancy** exit	(Page 35)
	Lighting on kids and on Bella's level L	
Cue 30	**Kids** exit R singing	(Page 35)
	Bring up lighting on O'Brien truck	
Cue 31	As Scene 13 opens	(Page 38)
	Change to somewhat stylized lighting—on two areas—kitchen and market place	
Cue 32	**Mary** enters and sees **John**	(Page 39)
	Lighting isolates them downstage C	
Cue 33	**Mary** and **John** go	(Page 40)
	Return to previous lighting	

Cue 34   As Scene 14 opens   (Page 41)
            Fade to lighting on kitchen—late evening

Cue 35   **John** goes   (Page 41)
            Lighting isolates **Mary Ellen**

Cue 36   **Mary Ellen:** "My God!" (*She laughs*)   (Page 42)
            Light on **Musician**, *light on back structure, light still on* **Mary Ellen**

Cue 37   **John** and **Mary** exit   (Page 42)
            Fade to light on **Musician**

ACT II

Cue 38   As Scene 1 opens   (Page 43)
            Lighting on Llewellyn drawing-room

Cue 39   As Scene 2 opens   (Page 45)
            Change to light on **Musician** *in back structure*

Cue 40   As snowcloths are set   (Page 45)
            Bring up exterior lighting, with bonfire effect off L *casting shadows*

Cue 41   Singing swells   (Page 49)
            Lights change—cut bonfire and shadow effect; bring up lighting on **John** *and* **Mary**

Cue 42   **John** and **Mary** kiss   (Page 50)
            Lights change; light on **Musician** *in back structure*

Cue 43   As lads strike snowcloths   (Page 51)
            Light isolating **Nancy Kelly** *in back structure*

Cue 44   As **John** and **Father Bailey** enter   (Page 51)
            Lighting on forestage—waterfront; fade lights on **Nancy** *and* **Musician**

Cue 45   As Scene 4 opens   (Page 52)
            Fade forestage lighting; bring up lights on **Musician** *and then on* **Nancy**

Cue 46   As O'Brien truck rolls forward   (Page 52)
            Bring up lighting on O'Brien truck, fade light on **Musician**

Cue 47   **Mary Ellen:** "... to have a bairn."   (Page 53)
            Cut Nancy's light

Cue 48   **Mary Ellen** and **Shane** go out to backyard   (Page 54)
            Crossfade to backyard area: lighting on various characters in back structure and levels

Cue 49   **Dominic** exits through the crowd   (Page 54)
            Snap lighting change, isolating the kids C, **Father Bailey** *and* **Peter** *in back structure, neighbours* DL, **O'Briens** R, **John** DR

Cue 50   **Joe Kelly** and two or three other men break over to R   (Page 55)
            Change to waterfront lighting DR

Cue 51	Adults part and form around **Joe** and **Hannah** *Crossfade from waterfront lighting to lighting on* **Hannah** *etc.*	(Page 55)
Cue 52	**Hannah:** "Joe, don't!" *Snap lighting change, isolating* **John** DR, *neighbours* DL, **O'Briens** RC, **Father Bailey**, **the Brackens**, **Musician** *and kids in back structure*	(Page 56)
Cue 53	When furniture for Scene 5 is set *Fade lighting on* **John** *and kids; bring up lighting on Llewellyns' drawing-room*	(Page 57)
Cue 54	**Mary:** "... does that make?" *Lights isolate* **Mary** C *and* **John** DR; *also* **Nancy** *in back structure*	(Page 59)
Cue 55	**Mary** moves DL *Light isolates her*	(Page 59)
Cue 56	**John:** "Mary ..." *Lights change to country at night*	(Page 59)
Cue 57	**Mary:** "Yes." (*She kisses him*) *Lights change, isolating* **Nancy** *in back structure*	(Page 60)
Cue 58	When ready for Scene 7 *Lights up on O'Brien truck*	(Page 60)
Cue 59	**John** and **Shane** exit *Crossfade to lights on* **Musician** *and* **Nancy**	(Page 63)
Cue 60	When ready for Scene 8 *Lighting concentrated on crowd facing upstage on harbour area*	(Page 63)
Cue 61	**Hannah:** "They're alive. Look." *Snap lighting change to crowd facing downstage*	(Page 64)
Cue 62	Crowd move down on to forestage *Lighting on forestage; light isolating* **John** *on back structure; swirling water effect in auditorium*	(Page 64)
Cue 63	All look and focus on where boat went down *Lighting to isolate* **David** *in* L *dock area*	(Page 64)
Cue 64	**John:** "Dominic!" *Light snaps up on* **Dominic** *on back structure* L	(Page 65)
Cue 65	**Nancy** takes **Molly**'s arm and takes her away, **Molly** in floods of tears *Change lighting as stackyard is set up*	(Page 65)
Cue 66	When stackyard is set up *Change to lighting on stackyard*	(Page 65)
Cue 67	**John:** "I'll find him." (*2nd time*) *Lights change as stackyard is cleared; lighting on back structure*	(Page 67)
Cue 68	When ready for Scene 10 *Bring up lighting on O'Brien truck*	(Page 67)
Cue 69	**John** holds **Mary Ellen**. They cry together *Light to isolate them*	(Page 69)

EFFECTS PLOT

ACT I

Cue 1   **Doctor** shakes his head and goes out front door   (Page 25)
Tape of kids chanting as script page 25

Cue 2   **Bella:** "She's soft her, soft as clarts." (*2nd time*)   (Page 25)
Tape of kids softly repeating "The O'Briens are fighting"

Cue 3   **Women 1,2,3** exit   (Page 26)
Tape of kids singing as script page 26

Cue 4   As Scene 10 opens   (Page 28)
Church organ music—fade after a few minutes

Cue 5   As Scene 11 opens   (Page 30)
Light classical piano music

Cue 6   **John** goes to sit, nervous   (Page 31)
Music stops

Cue 7   **Mary:** "I'll see you out." The Lights change   (Page 34)
Light classical piano music

Cue 8   **John** laughs. The Lights change   (Page 35)
Music stops

Cue 9   **Dominic** storms out front door   (Page 37)
Pause, then knock on next door

Cue 10   **John:** "Hey, come here ..."   (Page 38)
Loud banging of a door, off

Cue 11   As Scene 13 opens   (Page 38)
Tape of brass band and crowd singing "O Come All Ye Faithful"—fade when market is set up

Cue 12   **Mary** and **John** go   (Page 40)
Tape of brass band and cast singing "The Holly and the Ivy"—fade when ready for Scene 14

ACT II

Cue 13   As Scene 1 begins   (Page 43)
Tape of group of people singing "Auld Lang Syne", followed by music

Cue 14   Servants go   (Page 43)
Fade music

Cue 15	As Llewellyn furniture is struck *Tape of crowd round bonfire singing "Blaydon Races" off* L— *continue throughout scene, with snatches of other songs, as detailed in the following cues*	(Page 45)
Cue 16	**John** looks round at the crowd *Singing swells—"Waters of Tyne"*	(Page 47)
Cue 17	**Mary** walks slowly down to **John** *Singing fades*	(Page 47)
Cue 18	**John** and **Mary** go off R *Singing swells—"Bobby Shaftoe"*	(Page 48)
Cue 19	**Dominic** enters *Singing fades*	(Page 48)
Cue 20	**Christine** takes **Katie** and **David** by the hand and exits *Singing swells; then gradually fades as it transfers off* R, *becom- ing very faint and disappearing as next section begins*	(Page 49)
Cue 21	The Lights change. **John** remains isolated *Sound of deep, swirling water, continue*	(Page 64)
Cue 22	Huge gasp from crowd *Swirling effect changes to sound of water lapping gently— continue till end of scene*	(Page 64)
Cue 23	**John:** "Noooo!" *Optional echo effect*	(Page 64)

MADE AND PRINTED IN GREAT BRITAIN BY
LATIMER TREND & COMPANY LTD PLYMOUTH
MADE IN ENGLAND